GRIFF CARVER,

HALLWAY PATROL

GRIFF CARVER,

HALLWAY PATROL

JIM KRIEG

SCHOLASTIC INC.
New York Toronto London Auckland
Sydney Mexico City New Delhi Hong Kong

ISBN 978-0-545-28377-9

12 11 10 9 8 7 6 5 4 3 2 1   10 11 12 13 14 15/0

Printed in the U.S.A.   40

First Scholastic printing, September 2010

For my top cops,
Susan, Riley, and Dalila, with love.

CHAPTER ONE

HELEN NUTTING
GUIDANCE COUNSELOR
RAMPART MIDDLE SCHOOL

The following are portions of a TRANSCRIPTION of my recorded interview with student Griffin Carver, grade 7, recorded ██████████. This interview was requested by Beatrice Komack from the School Safety Bureau in conjunction with their investigation of the startling events of the last few weeks.

This was my first meeting with Griffin (I oversee 103 seventh graders alone!), and he was initially reluctant to talk with me at all. My telling him how much better talking about the situation would make him feel completely backfired. He said he had no interest in "feeling better." It wasn't until I stressed how difficult and painful the process was, yet how necessary to the public good, that we had a breakthrough.

NUTTING: Just pretend the microphone isn't there, Griff.

GRIFF: I'd rather pretend I'm not here.

NUTTING: Isn't there anything you'd like to get on the record?

GRIFF: (*shakes head distractedly*)

NUTTING: I'd think you'd want your side of the story told.

GRIFF: There is no "my side of the story." There's only the truth.

NUTTING: Why don't you tell me the truth, Griff? After all, I'm here for you. I'm a *pretty good* guidance counselor.

GRIFF: Really? Never seen you before today. Didn't even know I had a guidance counselor.

NUTTING: You know what, Griff? The sooner you talk to me, the sooner you're back out there in the halls doing what you're supposed to be doing!

GRIFF: I wouldn't even know where to start.

NUTTING: Start at the beginning. Your first day here. What was the first thing you saw?

GRIFF: Whattaya think I saw? The school. Same thing you see every day when you pull into the parking lot. Rampart Middle School.

NUTTING: Okay. What did you hear? Think about it. What was the first thing you heard when you saw the school?

GRIFF: "Have you got everything?" That's what she asked me. Something like that.

NUTTING: Then what? What did you answer?

GRIFF: "Yeah." I lied.

"There's nothing to be nervous about. Nothing at all."

That's what the Old Lady said next. She said it with a little squeak in her voice that let me know that she was nervous. Plenty nervous. I grunted at her, but she wasn't about to let up.

"Nobody knows anything about you here. You can start fresh. A clean slate."

The Old Lady pulled our gray minivan up another ten

feet as we waited our turn at the drop-off site. I looked through the window and got an eyeful of the place. I didn't know exactly what to expect from public school, maybe a bunch of little mobile homes for classes behind a serious chain-link fence. But Rampart Middle is old school. Big old main building with a playing field behind it and a lot of traffic in front. Hardly any graffiti. There's even a pool. But you know that. You work here.

And no, I wasn't nervous. Not really. The Old Lady was.

She was wound so tight, she didn't even notice the Go-Go's on the satellite radio. That was the sort of thing that usually sent her into some kind of a giddy New Wave flashback dance at the wheel. Not today.

"I know, Ma," I said, just to keep up the illusion of conversation. I knew the pep talk was really for her.

"Topschools.com rated Rampart Middle School in the top fifty safest schools in the state," she informed me, not for the first time. "So, really they don't need . . . There's no reason to—"

"Been through all this," I finally said. The car behind us honked and the Old Lady pulled up.

"Are you sure you've got everything?"

"Got my trumpet, got my new attitude . . . got my marching orders." Literally. The Rampart Middle march-

ing band was never going to be the same. I hadn't prac-
ticed since my underwear had Power Rangers on them.

"Got everything," I lied again as I slid out of the van
and dropped onto the sidewalk, loaded down with the
idiotic first-week-of-school flotsam and jetsam. All that
junk, but not the one item I gave a rat's butt about.

My badge.

"And Griffin!" she shouted after me. "Be careful!"

"Always am," I said, without looking back. I heard the
tic-tic-tic of the bad alternator as she pulled away and I
took in my new turf.

It wasn't ugly. At first blush, all you'd see is squeaky
clean kids playing and killing time till the bell rings. Big
lawn. Nice clothes. First-hand bikes. Right out of the
school brochure. Maybe that's all you'd ever see.

'Cause you never wore a badge.

Me? I carried that piece of tin for six years. Almost
half my life.

Started in first grade. Typical wet-behind-the-ears
rookie. Made all the rookie mistakes. Thought I was
God's gift to Safety Patrol. In retrospect, maybe I came
on a little strong. Like I was trying too hard. Like I could
do it all myself. Maybe I was asking for it. Maybe not.

Either way, I got it. The intersection of Maple Avenue
and Third Street. First graders were only supposed to

assist superior Safety Patrol officers, but somehow, probably to take me down a peg or two, I "accidentally" got assigned my own crosswalk. THE crosswalk. Mape and Three was the toughest intersection in town, a clearinghouse for third grade discipline problems who poured soda on their sugar cereal and had something to prove. That's where I learned what the red, reflective Safety Patrol belt did, the good kind that makes an X right across your chest.

It makes you a target.

You might as well draw a bull's-eye on your nose with permanent marker. Same effect.

What happened? You don't have to consult the Magic 8 Ball for that one. I got knocked down.

That's not the weird part. The weird part is . . . I got up again. And again. And again.

Too stubborn, or just plain dumb, to stay down. Maybe that's what makes me so good at what I do.

Did.

Don't know what you think of Safety Patrol. If you're like most people, you don't think about it at all. You don't know that the squad is the only thing holding it together. We're the thin blue line that keeps middle school from sliding into absolute and complete chaos.

Deep down, you probably know. Look at the sixth,

seventh, and eighth graders around you. The veneer of civilization will never be as thin as it is right now. Think I'm exaggerating? What did your class do the last time you had a substitute teacher? What did your hallways look like on the last day of school?

The patrol keeps order. Not much. But enough. Just enough.

And being a member of the Brotherhood of Officers makes me proud as . . .

Made. Made me proud. 'Cause that was all over for me . . .

"Watch out!"

A hand on my shoulder jerked me out of my brooding and onto the grass. Four BMX bikes shot past me in a blur. I was glad the Old Lady had already driven away. This was just the kind of near-miss scenario that sent her into hysterics.

The bikers laughed. Nothing quite so funny as a kid falling on his butt. Real comedy gem.

But it's better than being knocked over by eight Dura-Grip Flyers. Those were the tires. I got a close-up look at the brand as they rolled by my face. I asked for it. I lost focus.

"You okay?"

The first thing I saw was his shoes. They were shined.

Polished. I could see my reflection in those things. My would-be rescuer pulled me up to my feet, past the sharp creases in his olive pants, past the highly polished buckle on his camping belt, past the sash full of badges, the bolo tie. A real live Camp Scout. Lanky, fit, but with a smile so warm and trusting he gave you the feeling that he'd still expect a buck from the tooth fairy if he still had any baby choppers to stick under his pillow. The head-to-toe olive drabs didn't help much. Made him look like he was trolling for some old geezer to help across the street.

I know what you're thinking. Maybe they're required to wear their uniforms on the first day for school. Yeah, fine. Except this was the *tenth* day of school. My paperwork had just come through. The Camp Scout kept talking.

"You know, most cycling accidents occur within five miles of your home."

"No kidding?" I said flatly. "I'll tell my mom we need to move."

He had to think about it before he laughed. But at least he laughed.

"Good one," he said. "You're new, right? I make a point of knowing all the faces on campus."

FYI, when I start walking away, it isn't really an invitation to walk along with me, but that didn't stop him.

"Yeah, just transferred," I said.

"Lucky man," he announced. "You won't find a better, cleaner, or more secure school. We even have a pool!"

"So I've heard." Doesn't this kid have something better to do?

"And you're just in time for the Participation Fair."

At this point, I actually looked in his direction. "The what?"

Turns out, today I was not going straight to Homeroom. Nobody was. This was the day the entire middle school was funneled onto the football field for the annual Rampart Middle festival of "getting involved." Evidently, there's a school requirement for at least one extracurricular activity. Thank you, Parents' Association.

Camp Scout wasted no time in ushering me to the feeding frenzy. There must have been a "hospitality" badge in it for him somewhere.

He wasn't exaggerating. It was like a fair. Only without the puke-encrusted rides and two-strike carnies. Or the fun. Booths and tables for every club and wannabe activity. Latin, Chess, and Pep. Representin'.

I looked past the Plexiglas and neon stand for what must be the Science Club and saw a booth of tall, good-looking kids. I didn't even have to read the sign. I could tell they were student govie types. Some boy with a million-dollar smile was arguing with a serious girl with serious glasses. Even from this distance I was pretty sure that she was right and that she'd never get past that smile.

Finally, I eyed the booth with the large Marching Band sign over it. A few bandies, in full dress, were playing the crowd like a glockenspiel. They looked well funded and, as usual, full of school spirit.

"Well," I said in as friendly a tone as I could muster, "looks like my stop." I held up my trumpet case like a get-out-of-conversation-free card.

"Stay safe, kid," he advised me. Right out of the *Camp Scout Handbook*.

Once his uniform vanished into the churning sea of middle school identity-searching, I turned back toward the marching band booth. I almost took a step forward. Then, suddenly, I couldn't.

I just stood there staring at the bandies. What was my problem? They seemed happy. They were all friends. Probably went to band parties. Heck, they were better off than most. They'd come out of this extracurricular with a salable skill. Provided they could find someone to pay them to play, say, the sousaphone.

Come on, Griff. How hard could it be? You told the Old Lady you would. Promised her. And hasn't she been through enough? I lifted my foot to walk.

"Sure you wanna do that, son?" a man's voice asked.

I looked over and saw him. Coveralls. Mop. Garbage can on wheels with a few rat traps dangling from it. I don't know how old he was, but he'd been janitoring longer than I'd been breathing. "I wasn't doing anything," I told him.

"You were about to make a decision," he said. Like he knew. He had one of those voices. Gravelly. Like he had a line on *Wisdom* or maybe he smoked a lot, back in the day when people did that. It occurred to me that those two things were probably mutually exclusive.

"So?" I said.

He looked past me. I followed his gaze over to the bleachers. A lanky girl took out her chewing gum and affixed it to the bottom of the bench she was sitting on. Two boys were in a shoving match, the smaller one blissfully unaware that his opponent's buddy was creeping up behind him on hands and knees. One last shove and the sucker went toppling heels over butt thanks to the human stumbling block. Oldest trick in the book.

Literally. Some caveman learned to talk to his homey just so he could pull this stunt on a Neanderthal. Probably why we're still here.

"What do you see?" the custodian asked.

"Nothin'." I went with the standard middle school

response. He wasn't buying it. Meanwhile, the alpha shover was already victory-strutting away, victim's milk money in hand.

"What do you really see?" the old man persisted.

Maybe it was the nicotine vibrato in his voice or maybe he just caught me off guard by not buying my dumb-kid answer. Anyway, it all came tumbling out.

"An eighth-grade girl defacing school property. Two seventh-grade goons giving some dork the hi-low. Extorted milk money making its way up the food chain," I reported matter-of-factly.

And I was spot-on about the money. One piece of prime chuck had already handed it off to an eighth grader evidently suffering from gigantism, who quickly vanished into the crowd. I looked back at the old janitor. Was that a slight smile on his face? Tough to tell with all those wrinkles.

"You and me. We got something in common," he announced. "Everybody else looks over there and all they see is squeaky clean bleachers. But we know . . . there's a lot of dirt hiding underneath."

I glanced at his rat traps. "And maybe something more. Maybe something that scurries around, chewing up stuff that doesn't belong to him. Something that carries disease."

He nodded at me. Amen, brother. He glanced down at my trumpet case, then over to the band geeks. "Is that who you're gonna be here?" he asked.

I didn't give the man an answer. I don't think he was waiting for one. Instead, I just walked.

I walked past Drama Club. I walked past the Latin Society. I walked past the Athletic Boosters and Literary Junto.

I headed straight for it. I'd seen it out of my peripheral vision but hadn't wanted to look right at it.

No fancy booth. Just a lonely card table with a couple of the boys milling around. And one girl, of course, who was basically one of the boys. At least one of them had bothered to make a sign. Block letters in Magic Marker. Safety Patrol Squad. Nice recruitment work, fellas.

A round-faced kid a little older than me sat at the table. Not quite fat, but doughy enough to let you know that he spent a lot of time doing the paperwork. He looked tired. Tired of the responsibility. Tired of command.

"Not exactly turning them away," I said. "Need another hand, Captain?"

He barely glanced up from his textbook, titled *Algebra Is Fun-tastic!* His eyes didn't get any farther than the trumpet case.

"Band practice is every day during football season."

He sighed. "We can only take kids who totally commit."

Just then, the custodian walked by, rolling that oversize garbage can. Without any fanfare, I tossed the trumpet into his pail. That got their attention.

"Look like I'm afraid to commit?" It wasn't a question. The captain looked me over. If he was impressed, he wasn't gonna let me know. He picked up a clipboard and a pen.

"Name and grade?"

"Carver," I said. "Seventh."

"Experience?"

"Six years," I told him, "four on the street, two inside."

That nearly got a reaction out of him. It certainly impressed his guys. Junior crossing guards were relatively easy to come by. They're just as likely to drift off once they understand the grind and find out that the badge doesn't magically bestow the instant status and power they wanted. But an experienced Hallway Patrolman, that was something different.

"Where?" he asked, still not impressed.

"Saint Finbar's," I told him.

I saw the wheels turning behind his eyes. He looked up at me again, scrutinizing my face like I was a cousin he hadn't seen in a long time or maybe I had chicken pox scars.

"Carver. *Griffin* Carver?" he asked, suddenly interested. "*The* Griff Carver?"

"Heard of me?" I said. It wasn't really a question. But I'd been hoping my rep was a little more local.

"Dang," he said, "everybody's heard of you. Maple and Third. They still talk about that at Junior Police Camp."

"Who is this guy, Delane?" asked one of his guys. Doughboy shot him that why-am-I-surrounded-by-idiots glance.

"You don't know about Griff Carver, Dugan?" he taunted the poor kid. "Why does that not surprise me?"

"Griff Carver is famous." He said this to me, of course, not Dugan. "The only Safety Patrol officer in history to get kicked out of school." Then he waited. After a while I supposed that was my cue.

"Look, Captain," I started, "I don't suppose you care that it was all in the line of duty. If you look me up, you'll find my record was expunged by the school commissioner."

"I'll tell you what I care about, Griff," he said. "I care about the fact that five of my guys were eighth graders last year. They're all in high school now. Good for them, but I've lost half my manpower."

"Captain—"

"Delane," he corrected me, "and what I'm saying is,

you're experienced and I'm desperate. Got a little welcome-to-the-neighborhood present for you."

He reached into a metal lockbox on the table and pulled something out. He handed it to me.

The badge. Rampart Middle School Safety Patrol. Cheap plastic with a faux brass finish. A boxful probably runs less than ten bucks. It was attached to the rolled-up patrol belt with a rubber band. I unrolled the belt and put the rubber band in my pocket.

I am not exactly Mr. Emotional. Ask anyone, especially the Old Lady. But looking at that badge in my hand, my vision got blurry. For a second, I wasn't aware of anything else. But only for a second.

Delane smiled his fat captain smile. "Welcome to Rampart Middle School Safety Patrol, Griff Carver." He shook my hand. Not in any cool, kid way. He grabbed it straight on and pumped up and down, like your pediatrician.

I'd had enough commanding officers over the years to know that that's what they were. Politicians. Kids looking to score a few points on their magnate high school application. Of course, once they were on the job, it was more than they bargained for but too late to back out.

Right now, I didn't care about that. I was just happy to know who I was again. So happy I kept talking. Not like me at all.

"You won't regret this, Delane." I gushed like a green-as-grass rookie.

"Oh, I know I won't," Delane replied, already putting me in my place. "You're a loose cannon, Griff, and I'm keeping a tight rein on you."

I ignored the mixed metaphor, but my face had the question all over it. What did he have in mind?

"Think I'm letting a short-fused M-80 like you wander the halls *alone*, Carver?" he asked.

"No, no, no . . ." I stammered, terrified of his implication. He was going to team me up. "Captain, I never patrol with a partner. I work best solo."

"You patrol the way I tell you to patrol, or you don't patrol at all." Now he was really starting to sound like a CO. Well, it's never all good news, right? At least I was on the force. I'd be doing what I was made to do. So what if I had a partner for a little while. How bad could it be?

"Rodriguez!" Delane shouted out into the crowd. "Get over here! Now!" I couldn't quite make out the figure moving through the press of kids. "I want you to meet someone. Griff Carver, this is Thomas Rodriguez. Your new partner."

The red reflective patrol belt he was buckling on didn't do anything to cover up the sash full of badges or his platoon number. There was that spotless, pressed Camp

17

Scout uniform staring me in the face. I could barely see his moronically cheerful, courteous, thrifty smile from the glare off his shoes. Him. Why did it have to be him?

"Friends call me Tommy. Hit me . . . partner!" he said, holding his hand up for a high five. He'd be holding it up there for a long time.

CHAPTER TWO

RAMPART MIDDLE SCHOOL SAFETY PATROL
Incident Report

TO:
Delane Owens, Divisional Commanding Officer

FROM:
Thomas Rodriguez, Hallway Patrolman 2nd Class

DATE:
Monday, September 14, 8:10 a.m.

INCIDENT:
Near Collision at Stop, Drop, and Roll

At approximately 8:03 a.m. this morning, a seventh grade transfer student, Griffin Carver, was nearly struck by a gang of BMX bikers just after disembarking from a silver minivan at the Stop, Drop, and Roll site.

Delane, I know that you asked me not to file any more reports of incidents that *almost* happened, of "near misses," and I've made a serious effort to do just that. However, I'm making an exception in this case. First of all, the only reason the seventh grader was NOT struck by the first bike was because, acting purely on instinct and ignoring the personal risk to myself, I somehow managed to LEAP into the path of the bikes, GRAB the endangered pedestrian, and PULL us both to safety. I'm not looking for a "pat on the back" here, Delane, but just imagine what would've happened if I *weren't* there!

Second, the almost victim of this "pedal-by" is a new student. His first impression of Rampart Middle will always be colored by this moment of danger and thoughtlessness. I immediately did what damage control I could, stressing the safety record of the school, etc., but the damage was done.

Last, and most important, this near occurrence (as well as countless similar ones that go unreported) could've been avoided if we'd posted the YOU MUST WALK YOUR BIKE signs. As you know, I have made multiple requests for these signs without results. And, once again, I apologize for going "over your head."

I know that you believe these signs would be entirely ignored by the student body, but again I must, respectfully, go on record as disagreeing with your pessimistic and cynical viewpoint.

It's nice to know that *some* people (such as a certain *someone*, a personal friend of mine who is running for *class president*) DO think that there is room for improvement at this school.

RAMPART MIDDLE SCHOOL SAFETY PATROL
Incident Report

TO:
Delane Owens, Divisional CO

FROM:
Thomas Rodriguez, HP 2nd Class

DATE:
Monday, September 14, 8:35 a.m.

INCIDENT:
Addendum to Earlier-Reported Rear Collision

How funny is that? The very kid I save from being run over by the BMX gang ends up volunteering for Safety Patrol!

I don't want to toot my own horn, Delane, but I can't help thinking that I must've really made a good impression on the new kid! Not only did I save him from almost certain injury, but I also took the time to "talk up" Rampart Middle. If not for me, who knows what kind of impression he'd have of this place? Instead, now he's on the force!

Allow me to thank you for partnering me with Griffin. I think it demonstrates the great confidence you have in my ability to "show him the ropes." Don't worry, I'll have this rookie doing things the right way in no time.

Reams gave me a cryptic warning about Griffin. He said something to the effect of my new partner being the only Hall Monitor in history ever expelled from school. But I think that was just another example of Reams's "humor."

Reams is always "kidding me," I think, bcause he views my professionalism as being "uptight," and he's trying to help me "be cool." I knew better than to fall for his "jive" this time, but I will ask around about Griffin's history, just (a) to be thorough and (b) because it'll facilitate our inter-partner dialogue.

I'll let you know how it goes.

P.S. I was not thrilled when you threw away my earlier incident report as soon as you read the phrase "near collision." I'm sure you were simply swept up in the excitement of having a new recruit. So, I have taken the liberty of retrieving the report from the custodian's trash can and resubmitting it to you with this addendum.

CHAPTER THREE

HELEN NUTTING
GUIDANCE COUNSELOR
RAMPART MIDDLE SCHOOL

The following is a continuation of the RECORDED INTERVIEW with seventh grader Griffin Carver, which has been TRANSCRIBED professionally. When I asked Griffin to jump ahead and tell me about his experiences once he joined Rampart's Hallway Patrol, again he was unsure how to proceed. I suggested he try accessing a SENSE MEMORY. He requested (in colorful language!) that I explain this, and I told him he should pick an object present at the memory he was trying to recall, then re-experience the touch, taste, smell, etc., of that object. This technique, as you'll see, proved highly successful.

GRIFF: A cup of hot chocolate. Is that okay?

NUTTING: There's no right or wrong here, Griff. If that's the memory you picked—

GRIFF: (*interrupting*) There's *always* right and wrong, lady.

NUTTING: Uh—of course. I meant the cup of hot chocolate will work fine. Describe it to me.

GRIFF: I'm holding it in my hand. I can hear the tiny, pellet-like marshmallows tap against the side of the cup. I can feel the plastic Styrofoam squeak against my fingers.

And it wasn't hot, that's for sure. There are two things you should know about the Rampart Middle squad room snack table. There's plenty for everyone. And it's all terrible. The donuts tasted like papier-mâché, only less sweet and harder to chew. As for the hot chocolate, talk about false advertising. It was neither hot nor chocolate. But I suppose it was faster than saying "lukewarm sandy brown water."

In other words, it was pretty much like every other Safety Patrol snack table I'd ever run into. I guess that was only natural, since the squad itself looks pretty much like every other Safety Patrol squad. I'd seen a few of the guys already at that "join-up jamboree," but now, sitting in two rows of folding chairs in what they called the Multipurpose Room while Delane jawed away at an ancient lectern, I got a better look at them.

Maybe the squad attracts the same types in every school, or else certain traits are required for the job. Either way, they were all there. Reams, the clown who laughs at his own jokes. Dugan, the one with his hand up in the air every time he doesn't understand something— must have a pretty serious triceps from holding that arm up so much. Ciardi, who's just one of the guys, except for the supermodel hair and the fact that her first name is Gail. And "Meat" Mantling, the exception to No Student Left Behind. Like many a squad strong-arm, Meat would miss his original middle school expiration date by a few digits.

I'd seen them all before, or hall cops just like them. Me? From the looks on their faces, I'd say I defy easy categorization. They didn't know me from a hole in the wall. Speaking of which, there was a hole in the wall of the Multipurpose Room, at the base of the paneling on the far side of the room. In front of the hole was one of the rat traps I spotted on the janitor's pushcart, a fact I found more interesting than Delane's speech. I tuned out as soon as he mentioned Rampart's safety record. It was starting to feel like brainwashing. Two more times and I'd believe it myself.

I could tell by the tone of his voice, and the old clock on the wall, that Delane was wrapping things up. I felt joy mixed with dread. The joy: Just a few more minutes and I'd be back out in a hallway walking a beat. The dread: I'd be walking that beat with Tommy.

"Just remember, there's safety in numbers. We work as a group. There's no *I* in teammates," Delane continued.

"There's an *m-e*," suggested Reams, laughing. Dugan was about to raise his hand to ask for the joke to be explained, but Delane cut him off.

"You should always be checking your partner's six," Delane said. Then, with an exhausted look at Dugan, he added, "Which is the area right behind you. Remember, Dugan? It's like a clock? Your twelve is in front, your six is in back."

By now, the bell was ringing and the squad was rising, tossing their Styrofoam cups of lukewarm sandy brown water in the trash and adjusting their belts. But before we made it all the way to the door, we were stopped by Delane.

"Hey . . ." he called after us. "HEY! I don't want any *heroes* out there."

Every hall cop turned and continued on their way. *Yeah, I wouldn't worry about that, Delane,* we all seemed to say with a shrug.

The hallway floors of Rampart Middle are of ancient linoleum. They reflect the fluorescent lights a bit too well and give off a sickly sweet aroma of 100,000 swabbings with industrial-strength vanilla cleaner. The footfalls of endless students have carved rivers of erosion into their once flat surface. And, worst of all, they resound with the echoes of hard-soled shoes. The tac-tac-tac of Tommy's padded collar high-gloss chukkas drew attention to us in exactly the way I didn't like. It was our first patrol together, and I wasn't loving it.

His talking didn't help either. Mr. Helpful felt the need to narrate the patrol like a chatty tour guide.

"And there's the second-floor East Hallway drinking fountain."

I know it's a drinking fountain, genius. So, this is the second floor, huh? That explains those stairs we climbed. I didn't say any of that. I just thought it. Just because someone is a nimrod doesn't give you license to act like a jerk.

"Over here you'll find our state-of-the-art—"

"Science lab," I cut him off.

"Yeah, how'd you—?"

"The words *science lab* on the door were kind of a tip-off," I told him. I told myself that I'd made that sound chummy, not jerky. But who can say?

"PICK IT UP!" I heard myself shout. It was a reflex. The words were out of my mouth before I was even aware of what I had seen in my peripheral vision. It was the bounce of litter hitting the floor. A tiny piece of crumpled-up paper.

The litterbug was a middle-aged dude in a two-hundred-dollar suit from International Gentleman. And I don't mean he just grew old because time passed. This geezer had the look of a guy who'd been middle-aged since middle school.

"Excuse me?" he said, raising one white eyebrow.

Tommy tried to wave me off, to warn me away from hassling the faculty. He obviously didn't know me very well. "You just threw that paper on the hallway floor. *My* hallway floor."

"I don't know what you're talking about," he said, playing dumb.

"Right there," I said, pointing to the tiny piece of debris with my toe. "That's the wrapper from the straw in your iced coffee. You crumpled it up and dropped it there. It's still wet from the sloshing around you're doing. It's stained the exact color of your beverage."

Grandpa huffed and puffed for a moment, but he knew I had him. "I meant to put it in my pocket. It must have fallen accidentally."

"Then you won't mind picking it up, will you?" I asked. It wasn't really a question. Meanwhile, Tommy was wildly pantomiming to me from the other side of this guy. I made a mental note to pick Rodriguez in the unlikely event of a game of charades.

"Do you know who I am?" the dude asked. Took him long enough to bust out the diplomatic immunity.

"Let's see," I started. "You're too old for an eighth grader. . . . From your hair, suit, clean fingernails, the fact you're not carrying any books like a real teacher . . . and the fact that you're drinking a pricey iced coffee even though there's a complimentary machine in the faculty lounge, I'd say I'm talking to the principal. Clang? Or something like that?"

"Sprangue," he hissed. His face was red. I had to hand it to him, Principal Sprangue was an expert at keeping it bottled up. "What's your name, young man?" he asked in an overly calm manner that would've made me nervous if I'd bothered to think about it.

I opened my mouth to say, but he raised his hand to stop me.

"No, don't tell me," he said. "I'll find out everything

I need to know from Delane. I'm sure we'll be getting to know each other very well . . . Officer."

He turned and started to head toward his office.

"Principal Sprangue!" I called after him, unable to stop myself. He looked back and I glanced at the floor meaningfully.

It looked to me like his face was actually turning red, but that didn't stop him from bending over and picking up the straw wrapper before storming away.

"I'll be watching you!" he called from down the hallway.

When he was gone, Tommy fell against a bank of lockers like he was stunned. "No, you didn't!" he called. "You did not just nail Principal Sprangue for littering!"

"Nail him?" I asked innocently. "I politely requested he pick it up, that's all."

"I don't know whether to be amazed or appalled," Tommy said candidly.

The answer to that, evidently, was amazed, based on the fact that he wouldn't shut up about it. He was sure that Sprangue would find some way to exact revenge upon me.

As if the constant stream of words wasn't bad enough, Tommy made it worse by talking with a mouth full of peanut butter crunch Healthy Dude energy bar. I thought

I'd be able to get him to eighty-six the chewing, against regulations and all that, but no such luck. He had special permission to eat on duty for medical reasons. "I'm hypoglycemic," he said as he kept chewing and talking to me.

I would've asked him to put a sock in it (politely), but that would've been a distraction. I had new hunting grounds to memorize. I made a mental note of every stairwell and fire escape, noticed the locations of the poorly placed (and likely inoperative) security cameras, and got a feel for where the corridor traffic flowed and backed up. Important details, because they change at every school.

Unlike the students. The kids are always the same, instinctively splitting up into cliques of similar genetic information or social idiosyncrasies. In that giddy maelstrom between first and second period, we passed them all, locating their pods with a rapidity that defied normal human senses, banding together for that tantalizing illusion of safety in numbers. They were all there: the Jocks, the Straight A's, the Gamers, the Hair Girls, the Self-Imposed Outcasts, and the Student Govies.

This last group was out in force. Elections were coming up, and the campaigning was in full swing. Kids were handing out buttons, campaign stickers (where were they planning to stick those?), and even stuff like yo-yos with their names stamped on them.

"Vote for Creelman," someone mumbled at us as we walked by. Small voice for such a big girl. She held out a pamphlet. I couldn't tell if she was making eye contact with us because of the major-league prescription of her glasses, but I doubted it. Tommy took the literature.

"'Janet Creelman,'" Tommy read, "'the candidate for consistency and reliability.' That's her slogan? She's got to be kidding! Who's Janet Creelman anyway?"

"She is," I told him flatly, glancing at the girl handing out the campaign flyers. Her hair was like shoulder-length shag carpeting. I anticipated a long middle school experience for her.

"Oh," he said to me. "Sorry," he said to her.

"It's okay," she said. "But if you take the time to read the literature, you'll see I've defined six areas of potential improvement for Rampart—"

Janet's words were lost in a public roar of approval. Not for her, of course. There was another candidate kitty-corner from her. Despite being surrounded by a crowd, he was easy to spot. He was standing on a stepladder. At St. Finbar's, I would've run him in for reckless climbing, but I wasn't sure of the rules here, so I let it go.

"How long have you put up with this?" the boy on the

chair asked. He answered himself, "Too long!"

It was the Student Govie I saw back at the Get-Involved Fest. I never heard of any middle school kid having their teeth professionally whitened, and I'm not saying this guy actually did it, but judging from those dazzling, sunglass-inducing incisors, he just might've. He kept talking.

"*They* ask us to have school spirit, then give us homework on game nights! How are we supposed to support our teams *and* do hours of studying?! It's impossible! As class president, I will be a tireless champion of homework-free game nights!" Tooth whitening *and* speech classes. As the students cheered, I wondered when he was going to promise them video games in every desk and a moped at every bike rack.

A giant in a letterman jacket approached. Clearly, he had a local following, since the crowd started chanting, "Ni-no! Ni-no! Ni-no!" as he approached the ladder.

"Quiet!" he shouted, like he was calling a football play. The noise settled down and the gorilla, Nino, I presumed, spoke, or rather growled at the assembly.

"Marcus is okay," he said. "He supports the team and we support him. Vote for Volger." He just said it, no smiling or anything. Maybe that was for the best. Volger smiled enough for four.

"Vol-ger! Vol-ger! Vol-ger!" the crowd started chanting,

apparently spontaneously . . . but actually, I suspected, orchestrated by the Smile's inner circle.

We'd passed by him by this time, and the rumble of approval was already drowning out Volger's now continuing speech, which was fine by me.

"Now that's what I'm talking about," observed Tommy. I had no idea what he was talking about. My face must've told him so.

"I mean, that's a campaign I can get behind," he clarified.

I realized he was talking about the guy with the teeth. He was already off my radar. However, something else was on it. Footfalls. Fast and getting closer. Above the squeaks of runner's shoes I could hear the labored breathing. Everything was in slow motion. A girl being nudged to the side. Notebooks hitting the linoleum. I interrupted the Camp Scout.

"Incoming," I warned.

Tommy just looked at me blankly for a moment until the kid ran by. Then he got it. "NO RUNNING IN THE HALLS!!" he shouted. Uselessly.

My leg muscles tensed for action. Tommy just stood there. "Aren't we going after him?" I asked.

"Can't," he explained. "Rampart has a zero tolerance policy against running in the halls."

"Right. So let's go stop him," I suggested.

"Then *we'd* be running in the halls," Tommy said.

I don't shock easily. But lucky thing there were no flies in air at that moment, or one could've easily flown into my mouth, which hung open. Tommy got a little defensive trying to explain that he didn't make the rules, just enforced them. Really? That'd be news to me.

It got worse. Tommy started explaining modern Safety Patrol theory to me. Evidently, today's junior officer needs to be more than just an instrument of order. We have to be counselors, psychologists, friends, even, to the general student body. He pointed to a patch on his sash.

"This is a social dynamics badge," he told me, adding, "they don't just hand these babies out." I couldn't tell if that queasy feeling I was getting in the pit of my gut was Tommy or the hot chocolate I'd had an hour earlier.

"Hey! Slow down!"

This last item was shouted, by Tommy, at another hallway runner. By now, we'd made a circuit and looped around back to the main hall, where we started. Now, let's give the runner the benefit of the doubt and assume that he was deaf . . . at least to the shrill notes of Tommy's plaintive cry. I was climbing the walls inside my head.

"We really should do something about that," I offered

calmly, harnessing my questionable grasp of social dynamics.

"Oh, we do," he told me. "If you recognize the student, you can give him an official warning later. After three official warnings, which he can protest, he'll receive a yellow card, which—"

Another runner. I heard him early, my senses were so keyed up. As I felt the rush of air go past me, I didn't even look up. My backpack was off my shoulder instantly. I pivoted my arm around in a perfect arc like a seasoned bowler and let fly.

The knapsack glided across those highly polished floors like a weightless air-hockey puck. Its obvious heft returned, however, the moment it collided with the runner's ankle.

The crash was spectacular. He cartwheeled like a Hot Wheels Formula One across a deep-pile carpet, finally skidding on his flank into the Great Orator's stepladder pulpit.

The ladder toppled for a moment, nearly capsizing the boy atop it before settling down again. Instantly the ladder kid slid down the rails and roughly pulled the fallen runner to his feet by his shirt. For a second, just a second, I thought the ladder kid was going to take the runner apart. Then he looked up at me and Tommy . . . and smiled.

"Easy there, kid," said the smiling speech maker. "Perfect attendance isn't worth breaking your neck over." Somehow I doubted that was the runner's motivating factor.

The sign fell. The one that was being hung from the ladder. Amazingly, it was caught by two sets of hands before it even touched the Smile's admittedly awesome hair. MARCUS VOLGER FOR PRESIDENT.

Tommy finished filling out the official warning slip, ripped it off the pad, and handed it to the runner. "That's strike one, Nichols," he said unconvincingly. Nichols looked at the Smile like he was waiting for something, but all he got was, "Let's watch the speed from now on." It was a dismissal. "And vote for Volger!"

"Griff," Tommy said, "this is Marcus Volger, the coolest kid in school." Volger flashed that smile again as he laughed self-effacingly. "Hardly!" he demurred. Mr. Humble.

"Maybe not," I said, "but your campaign staff sure is working hard to make it look that way." I indicated the team of volunteers behind him, plastering Vote for Volger posters, handing out baked goods and bumper stickers that would never go on bumpers. Team Volger was mostly made up of normal-looking kids, if there is such a thing, but my eye went to two stocky boys who seemed to be doing a lot less work than the others. One was small eyed and large mouthed and definitely wasn't going to be handed a BE A TEEN MODEL! flyer at the mall. The other dude was like a huge slab of freckled meat ending in a shock of moss-like hair . . . if moss were red.

I wondered if my snarky comment got under his skin. I hoped so, but we were interrupted before I ever found out.

I smelled her before I saw her. Sugar and icing and everything nice. "Cupcake?" I heard a chirpy voice ask. It was one of Volger's acolytes, this one in a plaid skirt and anime T-shirt. She was offering me a mushroom-shaped explosion of milk chocolate with the words *Vote for Volger* written in frosting. Noticing my hesitation she added, "It's free."

Nice kid. "Nothing this sweet is ever free, cupcake," I told her. Somebody had to break the bad news to her, but I don't think she got it. She faded back into the crowd of zealots.

"Marcus was class treasurer last year," Tommy yapped on. "The zero tolerance policy on hallway running was his proposal."

"Nice rule," I lied, "except that we're prevented from enforcing the rule *by* the rule."

"You didn't seem to have any trouble enforcing it . . ." Volger observed. ". . . Griff, was it?"

I didn't smile or anything. I'm not that easy.

"Well, welcome to Rampart Middle," Volger said. There was that smile again. "And vote Volger!" You could still tell he was smiling even when he was walking away from us. Like his high beams were on.

"What's up with you?" Tommy asked as we continued down the hall. "Every kid in school likes Volger, Griff."

"Every dog in the world likes to drink antifreeze, too," I extrapolated. "Too bad it's poison."

"Really . . . ?" I heard. A girl's voice. A purr, really. And dripping with sarcasm. "Someone who isn't going to 'vote Volger.' And I thought it was going to be a slow news day." Clearly, I was right about the sarcasm. Good thing. I was beginning to think Rampart Middle had a zero tolerance policy for that as well.

There she was, standing in the doorway. I didn't have to read the name on the glass to know what room it was; I could tell from the smirk on her face. Tommy volunteered the information anyway. "Griff, meet the editor of the school rag—"

"Verity King, Junior Journalist of the Year," I finished. She arched an eyebrow. Pretty, but probably unaware of it. Not like I care, just a fact. I'd say the same thing to a police sketch artist. "We have the Internet back at St. Finbar's, too," I said by way of explanation.

She didn't like being in the dark. I could tell by the way she pushed her hair over her left ear. "Griff Carver," she said, just to see if there was a matching file in her head. "Seems to me I've heard that name before. Aren't you some kind of hero?"

"A hero's just a sandwich the cafeteria served us every Wednesday," I explained. "It was mostly baloney."

She exhaled to stifle her laugh. She liked sass, this one. Better go easy on the sass. I walked off. Tommy followed.

"Sweet!" Tommy yapped. "I've never seen anyone get the last word with Verity before." Bad enough he was talking. Then he had to keep talking. "She's actually kind of cute, really. You like her, Griff? You know, *like* her, like her?"

Tommy's body slammed into the lockers. Hard. But not too hard. I just wanted his attention, not a trip to the nurse's office. "Check it, Merit Badge," I explained, "we're not *friends*; we're not *buddies*; we're not *partners*. Delane said I had to patrol with you. He didn't say anything about *talking* to you!"

For a second, I thought he was going to explain to me the importance of an easy camaraderie between co-workers on a high-stress detail like hall monitoring. If he was, he never got the chance. Just then, the first-period bell rang.

The usual chaos of the hallway sped up like someone hit the FF button on their TiVo remote. As the kids scurried into their homerooms like cockroaches, I used the silence to let Rodriguez know how it was going to be.

"Come on," I told him, "we've got a job to do."

CHAPTER FOUR

HELEN NUTTING
GUIDANCE COUNSELOR
RAMPART MIDDLE SCHOOL

Continuation of the RECORDED INTERVIEW with seventh grader Griffin Carver.

GRIFF: Things got a lot more quiet after that. Big surprise, huh? But not just Tommy. With all the kids in class, the halls take on a cold, creepy feel, like you're the last guy on earth after an instantaneous worldwide pandemic.

Silence is one of the perks of hall duty. Giving up study hall three days a week and school assembly on Fridays is a small price to pay for walking a beat.

It's a lonely feeling and one I like. It's just you and the occasional kid en route to the can. You can tell they're aware of the creepy feeling too because they never talk to you. They see your belt, then just show you their hall pass and go on their way.

Slow day. We had three, maybe four kids on bathroom break. No one was sent to Principal Sprague's office. Finally, Tommy couldn't take that awesome silence anymore. He had to talk.

"Can't believe Delane assigned us hall duty," he complained. "At least at the bike racks we mighta seen some action! This is worse than being in class."

I almost felt sorry for him. I decided to throw him some Hall Monitor wisdom just to keep him from imploding from the lack of easygoing chitchat.

"Stay caffeinated, Rodriguez. Easy duty is twice as hard. The minute you get comfortable is when everything goes south."

"I appreciate the sentiment, Griff, I really do," said Tommy, "but it's been over eighteen months since we've caught anyone AWOHP in the corridor. That's—"

"Absent without hall pass, I know," I assured him. "So, Rampart is officially crime free, huh?" I asked dubiously.

"Well, we have an occasional incident," he countered

a bit defensively. "Like those BMX bikes this morning. I've found wet toilet paper wads on the ceiling of the boys' bathroom. And we've had a spate of false fire alarms this year."

"A regular reign of terror." I sighed. "Hall pass." That last part was not said to him. It was to another bathroom break kid. He handed me the pass.

Every school has different passes, even different philosophies behind the passes. They are all designed to be cumbersome and embarrassing enough to guarantee their safe return. My old, old school, where there were some security issues, handed out the actual bathroom key on a bent coat hanger, like a less reputable gas station. I'd also seen nice, colorful store-bought passes, laminated and with a decorative tassel. The Rampart Middle hall pass was an oversize hunk of engraved wood, like those paddles they have at fraternity houses (which, by the way, if they're actually used for spanking pretty much proves that people do not get smarter as they get older).

"S'up," he said. It wasn't really a question. He was simultaneously too friendly and too standoffish.

His pass was in my hand. But I wasn't looking at it. Reading a hall pass is boring. They're all the same. I was reading him. Stiff, staring straight ahead, pulling at the shoulder strap of his book bag.

I handed the pass back to Rodriguez without moving my eyes. "What's your name, kid?" I asked.

"I just want to go to the boys' room," he said. He hadn't answered my question. I took a closer look at him. He had straight dirty blond hair in the traditional bowl cut. I couldn't tell if this had been done by a cut-rate hairstylist or a cheap mom, but it was a little jagged, so I suspected the mom. He had dirty fingernails and the look of a kid who sharpens his pencil too long just to be annoying. But most noticeably, he had some kind of rash. Red skin poked up from under his collar, spreading onto his neck. Probably a long-term problem since he was used to covering it up. His long-sleeved shirt covered a lot of skin, but it was a warm day. Not hot, but fine for short sleeves.

"Name's Dover Belton," Tommy volunteered, proving his statement about remembering faces.

"Really?" I asked Tommy, but didn't wait for an answer. Instead, I asked Belton, "You always bring your backpack to the boys' room?"

Belton smiled weakly and shrugged. Keeping my eyes on the kid, I asked Tommy over my shoulder, "What do you make of his hall pass, Rodriguez?"

Belton's expression didn't change. He kept looking straight ahead, like he was bored.

"White oak," Tommy announced, turning the paddle

46

in his hands, "right kind of varnish, proper heft. Looks good to me."

There it was! I saw a tiny droplet of sweat drip out of Belton's hairline and across his temple. And, like I said, it was not that hot. Bingo.

"I don't think so," I said nonchalantly. Then, like a slap, I followed it up. "It's a fake."

"Wha—"

Belton sprinted down the hall before Tommy could get a shocked word out. The look on his face was worth all the easygoing camaraderie I'd had to endure before.

"How—how'd you know—?"

"We got a runner," I interrupted. "Let's go."

Just as I tensed to run, I felt a hand grab my arm. "The zero tolerance policy on running . . ." he started.

"Issue me a warning . . . later," I said as I wrenched my arm free and took off after Belton.

I won't lie. It felt great to tear down that corridor after a perp. The adrenaline was pumping, my feet were flying, and suddenly I remembered why I strapped the red reflective belt on in the first place. I was gaining on him.

I heard Belton's sneakers screech as he rounded the corner into a connecting hallway. He left marks on the school floor, but that was the least of his problems. I'd be on him as soon as I got around this corner . . .

I saw the blue liquid sluice across the linoleum. My mind knew it was the sports drink from the netting on Belton's book bag long before it could get the message to my feet to stop.

I instantly lost traction as soon as my sneakers hit the sports drink. I can't tell you exactly what high-fructose corn syrup is, but I can tell you that it's very slippery.

My inertia kept me moving forward as I slid through the supposedly "berry"-flavored thirst quencher and careened into a stack of eighth-grade lockers. The crash was so loud, its echo covered the relatively quiet thump of my body hitting the floor.

I looked up and saw Belton smirk as he dropped the empty squeeze bottle onto the floor. Pretty cocky of him to stop and gloat. I'd caught up to him easily and would do so again as soon as I climbed up to my—

Belton wasn't gloating. He was fiddling with the bottom of his sneakers. Why would he . . . ? Then I saw the wheel. He was fast. He had popped the wheels into both sneaker skates before I closed the distance between us. After that first push, his acceleration was impressive.

Now we had a ball game. I poured it on. I was breathing hard. I could hear my heart pounding against my ribs. The fastest I'd run since . . . it didn't matter. His wheels were faster than my feet. Belton got smaller and smaller in the distance.

My heartbeat was sounding louder. Too loud to be my heartbeat. Turned out to be footfalls, behind me. Suddenly, Tommy raced past me like a bullet train.

"You're slow, old man!" he shouted as he passed. I remembered the track-and-field badge on his scout sash. He could probably throw a discus better than me too, in the unlikely event that would become necessary in a high-speed-chase scenario. I don't think he was even sweating.

I slowed down. Maybe it was the new school. Or the move. Or everything that went down at St. Finbar's. Heck, who was I kidding? I'm in seventh grade—I'm not getting any younger. Maybe I'm past my best years as a hall cop. . . .

I was a dinosaur. Learned Hall Patrol from the old-timers, my brother and his pals, before they went to high school and everything went nuts. Guys like Tommy were probably the future. All those book smarts. And the obeying the rules down to the letter. Maybe he was using his head—

I stopped the pity party right there. He wasn't using his brains. He was using his legs. I was the guy who needed to use his head.

What would I do? On wheels. Being chased by a

Terminator. On the second floor. I'd be totally trapped. Or would I . . . ? Could he be that good?

I quickly reviewed the mental map of the floor plan I'd been assembling all morning. If he took the main stairwell, I had a chance. I turned into a small stairway and raced for the ground floor two steps at a time.

The main hall was deserted. I might have thought I was the only person on earth if it weren't for the student election posters. DI♥NNE FOR 6TH-GRADE SECRETARY! Like I'd vote for anyone who used a heart for the *o* in her name. Sorry, sister, it's a totally different shape.

I got my bearings and ran to the main stairs. Not all out. I'd need to be able to operate once I got there. My slower gait allowed my brain time it didn't really need. What if I was wrong? He could be anywhere. I had pretty good cop instincts once, but that was another school. Another lifetime. And look how that turned out. Maybe I was just fooling myself, even back then.

Then I heard him. I was just reaching the bottom of the stairs and there was a metallic crash echoing upstairs. Only one thing makes that noise. A school trash can slamming against the floor as it spills across the laminate.

I heard Tommy cry out. Even from downstairs, I knew he'd tripped over the garbage that Belton had used to block his path. He was good. And he'd be coming down those stairs any second.

And I didn't have anything. Except maybe surprise. Duh. Wake up, Griff!

I threw myself against the wall at the base of the stairs, out of sight. Just in time, the staccato scatting of Belton's wheels bouncing down the steps got louder and louder. And fast! What was this kid? In the X Games?

I only had seconds and, as usual, I was unarmed. I felt a fleeting sympathy for English bobbies. "Stop! Or I'll blow my whistle again!" Unless . . .

I reached into my pocket. The rubber band, the one from the patrol belt, was still there. I pulled it out and looped it over the tip of my right index finger and stretched it across the heel of my thumb, pinning it to my palm with my middle finger. Instant slingshot finger gun.

Only one shot. Better make it count. I steadied my arm with my left hand and pressed myself closer to the wall.

There was his shadow. He reached the bottom of the stairs, home free. Or so he thought.

I heard the wheels. It was now or never. I stepped out.

It happened so fast. I'm kind of amazed his face even registered my presence as I raised my hands, left hand steadying right wrist, and pointed my finger at him. Surprise.

I shot. No warning. The rubber band was off my finger instantly. Belton's hands automatically flew to cover his face, but that wasn't where I was aiming.

The rubber hit his shin at 11.71 mph. No permanent damage, but I can tell you from personal experience, it hurts. He made a satisfying yelp and gripped his leg. He still had plenty of speed as his wheels lost their connection with the ground.

The wipeout was spectacular. I could've sold tickets. After hitting the trash can, the twin of the one he'd knocked at Tommy upstairs, he careened past me, across the hall, and into the empty table of election baked goods. I'd love to say that it was still full of frosted cupcakes when Belton smashed into it, but life is never perfect.

But as Hall Patrol moments go, this was pretty darn close. I walked over to him shaking my head. He was rubbing his.

"Let's go, Hot Wheels," I said matter-of-factly. The perp doesn't need to know that he's an awesome bust. He needs to think you do this all day, every day.

"Uh-uh . . ." he stammered, on the verge of tears. "No way. I—I can't get detention, man. Please!"

Everyone reacts differently to getting busted, and you've got to be prepared for it. Belton's reaction was pretty typical. Panic. He'd beg, weep, do anything to get out of that long walk to the principal's office.

"Come on, man! I can help you!" he pleaded.

See what I mean? "Oh, yeah?" I responded. "Help me how?"

"I can hook you up," he told me. The tears were gone, replaced by the hopeful grin of a desperate salesman. "What do you want? Otter Pops? Baseball cards? A note for gym? From a real doctor? I'm the man, G."

I had to hand it to Belton. If he didn't end up in jail, he'd probably be great at selling stuff someday.

"I don't need anything," I said, to shut him down. He pulled out the big guns.

"Test answers," he suggested, his voice much lower. "English papers, finished homework."

I pulled him to his feet, but not too roughly. He could see that he'd piqued my interest.

"You're a busy man, G.," Belton said, suddenly my best friend. "Why waste time with all that busywork? They can't expect you to risk your neck out here in these mean corridors *and* do math homework with fractions."

I winced. He probably noticed that he'd hit a soft spot.

"My old man's always on my back about the math grades," he confided.

"I don't have an old man," I admitted, "but my mom . . ." I made a face to indicate just how nuts she was over my grades. No lie there. He smiled.

"I totally commiserate with you," he said.

"You can't help me," I said flatly.

"I'm telling you," said Belton. "I'm connected. I run with this crew. We own this place. Always looking for guys who know how to handle themselves."

"Tell me more," I said.

CHAPTER FIVE

RAMPART MIDDLE SCHOOL SAFETY PATROL
Incident Report

TO:
Delane Owens, Divisional CO

FROM:
Thomas Rodriguez, HP 2nd Class

DATE:
Friday, September 18, 1:07 p.m.

INCIDENT:
Supplementary Information to HP Carver's Report

After reading Hall Monitor Carver's IR describing Tuesday's high-speed chase, I feel compelled to submit my own version of the incident.

In essence, most of Carver's report is pretty accurate, if short. Like many of my fellow officers, Griffin does not seem to understand the importance of good paperwork.

But even the fact that I did, in fact, temporarily ignore the school's no-running policy is pretty much true. That I was caught up in the "heat of the moment" in no way excuses my totally uncool behavior. I'm willing to accept whatever disciplinary action you deem fit, Delane, but keep in mind that (a) I am already being punished by my own conscience and (b) Safety Patrol is terribly understaffed this year.

However, you should be aware that a few key details, either by oversight or subterfuge or whatever, have been omitted from Carver's report. Both my duty and the fact that I consider us "buds" compel me to fill in the holes.

Despite his Heelys, I was gaining on the fleeing suspect (whom I believe to be Dover Belton, student ID #8376394) at an acceptable rate. As you know, I pride myself on my acceleration in a sprint as well as my endurance over long distances.

As we reached the east end of the upstairs hallway, the sun from the big window hit me right in the face and I was temporarily blinded. At just that moment, the suspect grabbed the large trash receptacle at the top of the stairs and yanked it over. The can's top opened and the contents (mostly paper, contraband candy wrappers, and soda bottles) spilled across the corridor toward me.

As I mentioned, my speed was impressive. So when I hit that spilled garbage, I went flying. The loud clanging sound was my first indication that I'd collided with the trash can. The physical pain I felt hitting the floor was another indication.

By the time I sat up and looked over the trash can, the suspect was already more than halfway down the stairs, a pretty impressive feat on skates. Despite his lead, I climbed to my feet and raced after him, which I'm sure does not come as a surprise to you. You have often complimented me on my single-minded determination. At least, I *think* those were compliments.

Hurrying down the stairs, I heard a yelp of pain, then voices talking in low but emphatic tones. I was just rounding the corner when I caught a glimpse of the aforementioned HP First Class Carver pulling the suspect out of the remains of a collapsed folding table.

Griff had somehow guessed where the perp was going to run and beat him there. I was pretty impressed. Maybe his reputation is more than just hype. With the action over, I slowed down to a walk. Now I had all the time in the world to stroll over and pat Carver on the back for a job well done.

Well, maybe not literally "pat" him on the back. HM First Class Carver has a strong sense of personal space. Not exactly a team player.

". . . This never happened . . ." At least that's what I think I heard. It was Griff's voice. I slowed down, hoping to hear more, to figure out what was "going down" here. I ducked behind the edge of the stairwell and strained to hear the conversation.

"Now get lost before the deputy Camp Scout shows up," Griff said. THAT I heard. No mistake.

"Y-you won't be sorry, man," Belton stammered. Then I heard footsteps and decided it was time to make an appearance. But I didn't just step out of my hiding place and walk up. No, I *jogged* up to Carver, puffing like I had just run down the stairs. I was pretty convincing. As you know, Delane, I also have a dramatics badge.

I didn't see Belton (or whoever he was) anywhere. Griff looked up at me, but I couldn't read his face. Was he scared, excited, nervous? Who knows?

"What happened?" I asked. Again, I was very naturalistic.

"Nothing," he said. "He got away from me, that's all."

Wow, he was totally lying to me, but I only knew that

because of my sneaking and eavesdropping. If I'd just been talking to him, instead of secretly testing him, I'd have believed the guy.

I pointed down the corridor. You could hear the sound of Belton's running feet getting softer and softer. "That's probably him," I said. "We can still catch him."

I was just about to run after the sound when Griff caught my arm and stopped me dead in my tracks. Yeah, it kind of hurt, but nothing I couldn't deal with. "That's not him," he told me matter-of-factly.

"Let's catch him and find out," I said accusingly.

"I told you," he almost growled, "that isn't him. Let it go. That kid's long gone by now."

I sensed something was really wrong here. My famous Hall Monitor instincts were going haywire. But I wanted to give a fellow officer the benefit of the doubt. Just then the class bell rang. The classrooms were about to burst open. I thought I'd better give it one last try.

"If you ask me, it's our duty to make just one more round of the halls and see if he turns up anywhe—"

"I didn't ask you," he interrupted. He stared me in the eyes, threateningly, like *You better forget this whole thing ever happened, kid.* At least, that was my impression. I know that wouldn't hold up under a disciplinary review or anything.

Suddenly, kids were pouring into the hall. I turned back to Griff. I wanted to give him one last chance to level with me.

He was gone. Like Batman.

P.S. I wanted to end there, Delane, but I should clarify what I meant. You know how when Batman is talking to someone and they look away for a second and when they look back, Batman has disappeared mysteriously? That's how Griff took off. It was just like that.

It got me to thinking about how, if you wanted to pull that off, you'd have to always be waiting for the person you're talking with to look away so you could melt into the crowd or the night or what have you and it would be really hard to keep up your end of the conversation.

CHAPTER SIX

Dear Diary,

I cannot believe I just wrote that. I feel like I'm going to throw up. Seriously? "Dear Diary"? Who am I? Holly Hobbie? Polly Pocket? Laura Ingalls Wilder?

Okay, maybe I'm a little out of line, lumping Laura Ingalls Wilder in there. She was a real person, not a doll specifically targeted at impressionable young girls. For all I know, she didn't even like pink. And I should really cut her some slack for freezing her butt off on that godforsaken prairie.

Well, Diary, what do you think of my first entry? Can you tell that I'm just writing to look like I'm writing? Are you somehow aware that Aunt Dede is sitting across the living room with her English Breakfast tea? Can you feel her smile every time she looks up at me and sees that I'm actually writing in this thing?

"Oh, look at this *darling* little diary!" she must've said when she saw you in the store. "Verity would just adore you! She's *quite* the little writer, you know!"

I have to hand it to my mother. She's a pretty amazing nonverbal communicator. With one look she told me, "I don't care how pink and girly that diary is, you start writing in it *now*! You do it in *front* of my sister. And you *keep* writing in it until her visit is over or you can kiss the Internet goodbye for the foreseeable future."

That's a lot of information to deliver with one eyebrow raise. I guess there's still a thing or two she can teach me.

Okay, hideous pink-lined paper with the kitten in the corner, what now? Mom and Aunt Dede are still yacking away, so I'd better think of something to write about.

Tell you about my day? Why, sure! I'd love to. Mr. Button made me rewrite my piece on Spirit Week. He said it was a little flat. Really? My article on float building and pep rallies was a little been there, done that? Excuse me! It's still better than anything Tia Summers would hand in, and you'd pat her on her head and say, "Nice work, Tia!" And you know what? Telling me I'm capable of more than other students in no way makes up for the fact that I have to do the whole thing over.

Oh, and I might have a story. A real story, on the off

chance that Tommy isn't just talking because he's . . . well, being Tommy.

I noticed him in the cafeteria today, just standing there looking like he'd swallowed something horrible, for instance, anything produced in that cafeteria, as I was giving the Apathetic Five their marching orders.

"All right, listen up," I announced to my alleged team. "Nino Coluni just got suspended from the team. That makes a noise like news. Talk to me."

"Nino Coluni, the captain of the football team?" asked the brilliant Ms. Summers.

"Yes, Tia," I answered, trying to keep the snarky attitude out of my voice, "*that* Nino Coluni. Not one of the many other Nino Colunis we have wandering around here. What's the story?"

"Heard he blew a Spanish test big time yesterday," mumbled Gustafsson. "That was the tipping point to academic probation. Coach had to bench him."

"That's what you *heard*, huh?" I responded. "Too bad I can't run what you ' *heard*.' I want quotes, sources, and statistics. What does that lunkhead need to get on the next test to get back on the field?"

I couldn't help notice that Tommy was still hovering around looking like he'd just swallowed a yogurt pop without checking the date on the tube. No, he looked worse than that. He reminded me of Quentin Brody just before he asked me to the Halloween Hop. A for effort, Quentin!

Then I knew. Tommy had something for me.

"I know that face," I told him. "That's a face of someone with news."

Tommy's eyes darted over the AP 5. Whatever story Tommy had to tell, it wasn't public information. Needless to say, that's when I suddenly became interested.

"You're busy," he said. "It can wait."

If you're going to be my diary, there are some things you're going to need to know. For example, the first rule of journalism: The news *can't* wait.

Neither could I. "Bernstein, six hundred words on the football team's prospects without Nino. Gustafsson, I want those facts, and Johnson, editorial on Sprangue's broken promise of more sixth-grade lockers. The rest of you, find news."

My crack team lumbered to their feet and, after a particularly long interlude of chair squeaking and cafeteria tray collisions, raced off to their assignments with the speed and alacrity of a herd of aging, underfed oxen.

"You didn't have to blow off your friends," Tommy said.

"What friends?" I asked. "They're reporters. I'll make friends when I get to high school. Right now I've got a paper to run."

Now, Tommy's a bit touchy about our arrangement, so I thought better of ending on business. So I grinned and added, "Besides, it's Beans 'n' Franks Day. Best to get rid of them before the gasworks start up."

Tommy laughed so hard I thought I was going to have to take him to the nurse. When dealing with boys, it's always a good bet to go with the scatological material. They can't get enough of it.

I wasn't entirely kidding, either. Seems like every other Tuesday there's enough natural gas in the cafeteria to supply the nation's energy needs for the foreseeable future.

"What is it, Tommy?" I asked. "Spill."

"What if . . ." he started, "*hypothetically* . . ."

Hypothetically? I didn't even know Tommy knew the word *hypothetically*. Good for me. First rule of journalism: *Hypothetically* always means "this is absolutely true, but I don't know if I should tell you." This is the kind of stuff that I love.

". . . I knew something about somebody. Somebody who's supposed to be so great, but . . . you found out he wasn't great at all."

"Who is it?" I asked. First rule of journalism: Cover your W's . . . who, what, when, where, and wow. I substitute *wow* for *how*, Diary, because it drives me nuts that one of the Ws starts with *h*. I mean, come on!

"Hypothetically," he said, rather defensively, I thought.

"Hypothetically, you'd tell me," I reminded him. "And I'd put it in the *Liberty Bell*, like always."

This may have been a misstep by me. Tommy is touchy about our arrangement, but I don't know why. How many times do I have to explain to him that the students of Rampart Middle have a right to be informed of all relevant information that pertains to them and not to be spoon-fed only those facts the powers-that-be deem "appropriate"? Also, he has every right to a passing grade in English, and if I *choose* to tutor him, that's just me helping out a friend and nothing nefarious.

Tommy sighed. What was the problem? Why wouldn't he tell me what he knew? Or at least who he knew it about? Then it hit me.

"You'd tell me . . . *unless* it was someone on Safety Patrol."

I saw Tommy's face change color, calling into question his future as a professional poker player.

Wait a minute! Did that mean what I thought/hoped/

prayed it did? A bad hall cop? Hallelujah! Please, yes! What a story!

"Maybe this was a mistake," said Tommy, getting all antsy and fidgeting to leave. This was the dangerous part, if he bolted before I had him.

"It's the blue wall of silence, right?" I asked.

Tommy stared at me blankly, and by that I mean more blankly than usual. He didn't know what I meant. I've learned that part of my job as a journalist is to be an educator.

"The unspoken code of honor among Safety Patrol officers where they refuse to inform on one another," I explained, adding pointedly, "*regardless* of whether it's the *right* thing to do." Emphasis mine. Because that's how I said it.

Tommy's eyes darted away from me, but I got the idea that it was not just out of avoidance. He was looking at something, so I followed his gaze to the exit side of the cafeteria. Yes, there's an IN door and an OUT door, to control the flow. Feng shui from 1961.

Someone was coming in. Yes, through the exit, but not in the clueless "Oh, is this the wrong door?" way. It was a boy whose walk delivered an unspoken dare: "Yeah, I came through the wrong door, what are you going to do about it?"

"It was Griff Carver."

"It's the new guy!?" I blurted out, my reporter cool totally blown for the moment. "The *hero?*" This was too much! This new Hallway Patrolman had only been in school a week and everyone already knew him. Not that he said much. But he was hard not to notice. I'm not saying he's cute, which I guess he could be. The girls noticed him, but I don't think it was because of his *Popstar!* magazine cover-worthiness. It was his intensity. When this guy was on hall duty, you felt his eyes on you. Even when he wasn't looking right at you.

"I didn't say that!" snapped Tommy, his future as a professional poker player now nonexistent, as far as I was concerned. But now I was on dangerous ground, and this next part had to be played just right. If I pushed too hard and scared him off, I would rue the loss of this story the way Bianca Fuller regretted her ill-timed break-up with Tad Shore just before the yearbook staff voted on "cutest couple." Some disappointments you don't just snap back from.

I instantly retooled my mental headline SAFETY PATROL LEGEND LEADS DOUBLE LIFE OF CRIME into something more persuasive. "Tommy," I asked, "do you have a picture of yourself that would go well with a *hypothetical* headline like HERO HALL MONITOR ROOTS OUT CORRUPTION?"

"Yes," he said, picturing the front page.

"The Tommy I know," I continued, "would never let some archaic tradition get in the way of his unswerving loyalty . . . to *justice*." I said it just like that, too, with the pause for effect. "Am I wrong about you?"

"No," answered Tommy, his little chin tightening in determination. "You're not."

"Now listen, Tommy," I said putting my arm around him conspiratorially. "We're gonna need proof. Mr. Button won't let me print a story like this without it. He may be the coolest teacher, but he's a stickler for proof. That's where you come in, understand? Make no mistake, a story like this is huge. It could do really good things for us, or it could blow up in our face, like . . . lighting a match on Beans 'n' Franks Day."

Aunt Dede's getting up! Thank, you Lord! I only have to write a little bit more in this flowery atrocity! That's it, look how much Verity loves your gift. Verity writes so quickly! Say goodbye to Mom. Put your coat on. Ah, here you come to kiss me goodbye . . .

Goodbye!

CHAPTER SEVEN

RAMPART MIDDLE SCHOOL SAFETY PATROL
Incident Report

TO:
Delane Owens, Divisional CO

FROM:
Thomas Rodriguez, HP 2nd Class

DATE:
Monday, September 21, 2:41 p.m.

INCIDENT:
Cafeteria Surveillance

You know, officially, Delane, I probably should've come right to you with my suspicions about Carver. I guess it has something to do with the blue wall of silence. And by that

I mean how us hall cops don't tell on each other unless it's a really big deal. Which it is. Don't feel dumb if you don't know that expression. A lot of kids our age have never heard it before.

So, after a few days of solo time, completely by myself, considering this whole mess, I came to the conclusion that I needed to investigate further. I mean, you wouldn't expect me to move forward without proof, right?

Well, I was in the cafeteria, mulling this over in my head, alone, when there was a small disturbance at the exit door that my acute cop internal radar immediately became aware of. Someone was coming in the out door. I was already reaching for my pad to issue this scofflaw an official warning (or, hopefully, he was a repeat offender and I could stick him with a demerit), when suddenly, I recognized him.

You guessed it. Carver.

What is it about this guy? The crowd of kids just kind of part for him. Not like they're afraid of him, exactly. More like he radiates a sense of being on "official business."

I was so focused I didn't even say goodbye to Verity.

I mean, I didn't even say *hello* to Verity when I passed by the table where she was holding court with her reporters as usual.

As you know, the routine chaos of Rampart's cafeteria makes for great cover. I melted into the pandemonium and, gauging Griff's trajectory, made my way toward what looked to be his destination. Guess where he was going.

Give up?

Forget it. You'll never guess in a million years.

Marcus's table. Yes, Marcus Volger's table.

I know, right? What's he want with Marcus? To my knowledge, they hardly know each other. I introduced them that first day when I was showing Griff the ropes. Then we ran into Marcus a couple times when we were on class-time monitor duty (Marcus must have a tiny bladder or something, but do not say that to anyone!).

Seriously, what did a once-expelled, dirty Hall Monitor like Griff Carver have to say to a squeaky clean populist like Marcus Volger? Of course, there was no way to know . . . for anyone without extensive surveillance experience.

Marcus owns that table. Everyone there is a FOM (friend of Marcus). Big Ben Gave was sitting with him, of course. And so was Morgan Boca with his million freckles. I knew my visible presence would negate any interesting and revealing conversation. The extensive required reading I did to earn my espionage merit badge led me to believe that I needed to vanish.

Thankfully, I had my Spy Bling gear with me. I know, I know. You and I don't see eye to eye on the value of this versatile and effective set of play equipment from

Clandestoys®. (Toys? Yeah, right!) Rest assured this is not another requisition for Night Vision Extreme! binoculars.

As I casually walked toward Volger's table, I "accidentally" dropped a quarter on the cafeteria floor and disappeared from view as I bent to pick it up. Of course, I didn't pick it up. And it wasn't a quarter.

It was a Spy Bling covert listening coin, which I expertly rolled through a constantly shifting obstacle course of moving feet before it came to rest under Marcus's table. All that was left for me to do was to tune in on my receiver and earpiece (which looks like an MP3 player, kind of) and pretend I was looking for a cool enough table.

"Hallway Patrolman Carver. We meet again." That was Marcus. It was a little staticky, but that's just the sort of thing he would say.

"We meet quite a bit, Marcus," Griff answered. "In fact, you're in the hallway a *lot*. More than any other kid I know."

The static let me know that I'd have to inch my way closer in order to be where the action was. And if I wanted to stay invisible, I only had one option: Go low.

"That's not a crime, is it?" Volger asked through the fuzz.

"No," Carver agreed, adding, "not when you have proof of

permission, like you always do." This must have been some kind of small talk, so no big deal that I didn't get it all.

There was a loud SQUEALCH in my ear and I lost them completely for a while. Casually moving as close as I dared, I then convincingly pantomimed having to tie my shoe (again, dramatics badge), scurried under the adjacent table, and tuned in the bug.

Finally the static cleared and I could hear them again. "Your boy here thought we could make some kind of deal," Griff's voice crackled over the earbuds. He sounded different. And it wasn't just the static. The word *deal* dripped heavy with vice.

Let me just add here that the table I was using as cover was NOT empty. There were a lot of sixth graders at it, and they were a fidgety bunch, believe me. More than a few had the jimmy leg, and there was more than one near-collision between my head and their shoes. Not that I'm uncomfortable with a high-stress situation.

"Belton? I barely know him," answered Marcus. Voice sounded totally normal. "He's just a kid on my campaign team. There are a lot of kids campaigning for me. I can't be held responsible for every random comment made by each and every one of my supporters."

A wave of static BLEW OUT my ears. And that wasn't the worst of it.

It was Beans 'n' Franks Day. At the table above me, kids were shoveling down pinto beans and sliced hot dogs like it was the best thing they'd ever had. The gas was starting in earnest.

"Well, it's like this," Griff went on. "There's always some smart kid who's got the school wired. Not a spit wad gets shot, not a dweeb gets pantsed without his okay. A puppet master."

Another bout of static washed away their conversation. I suspected that several kids at the table above me wore braces, and every time they opened their mouths, I was hit with interference.

What was Griff getting at? Was he making some kind of claim to the throne of Rampart Middle's underworld kingpin? And why tell Volger, anyway? Maybe he was trying to warn him, in case Marcus won the election, that he'd better not mess with Griff. I found it hard to focus my thoughts, the noxious gases were getting so thick down there. Didn't know how much exposure my body could withstand, but I had to hear more. I could just make out Griff's voice through the static and the building waves of nausea.

"A smart kid might find it helpful to have a hall cop on his side. A guy who'll look the other way, tell him when the heat's on. For a price. A guy like me."

Air . . . almost gone. But had to hang on . . . Had to figure out what Carver was saying . . .

"Griff, I can't speak for my friends here," Volger responded, apparently baffled, "but I don't understand what you're implying."

My head was swimming. I had to focus. Use the intense concentration I have mastered as part of that after-school study techniques course. But it was so hard. . . .

"However," Marcus added, in what I thought was a weird, low tone, "we're always looking for new friends. Who knows? And don't forget: Vote for Volger."

Through the moving forest of legs, I could see Griff turn from the table and walk away. Finally! My lungs were at the breaking point. If I hadn't suffered any brain damage from lack of oxygen, it would happen soon enough.

Then, agony. Griff's legs stopped, and I saw him bend down to pick up the covert listening coin!!

"Twenty-five cents," I heard him say, loud and clear. Then he added, "Five more of these and I can buy a candy bar."

His legs walked away. My high-tech equipment, which I paid for myself, was along for the ride.

My throat and lungs were burning, my eyes were watering, and my nose? Let's just say I never want to smell anything ever again. If not for my Camp Scout discipline combined with my own personal high pain threshold (just ask my dentist!), I wouldn't have made it. I don't think anyone I know would've lasted as long as I did. No offense, Delane.

I burst through the legs of the flabbergasted gas factories (on the opposite side of the table from Marcus, natch) and scrambled for air.

Stumbling through the cafeteria, I knew three things for certain: The no matches and/or lighters on campus rule had saved my life. An ill-timed open flame would've meant a massive fireball. The administration needs to rethink Beans 'n' Franks Day. The ability to hold one's breath is vital to an officer. I must continue to practice this on a daily basis.

Griff was up to no good. I didn't know what his plan was or how I would stop him. I knew only that I could not allow him to pollute my school nor disgrace the red belt and sash of the Rampart Middle School Safety Patrol.

If you've been reading this incident report *closely* and not skimming it (which, by your own admission, you have done in the past), you will have noticed what I didn't do in the cafeteria. If you guessed "eat lunch," you are 100 percent right.

I had put my devotion to duty above my own physical and practical needs. That's just how I roll. However, I also know that in order for the human body to operate at peak efficiency, one has to ingest sufficient calories. If I find myself in class, groggy and sluggish from lack of food, I'm not justifying the student body's trust in me. They deserve better than that.

Which is why I found myself at the west hall snack machine two periods later, trying to insert my dollar into the bill slot. The machine wouldn't take my dollar, can you believe it? Not the first one, or any of the others I tried to jam in there. Which is surprising, since I always make a point of carrying only clean bills with few wrinkles and no tears.

I was just jotting down the 1-800 customer service number in the notepad I always keep in my breast pocket when I heard a voice say, "Even if they send you a check, how's that going to help you now?"

It was Marcus, taking a break from the campaign trail. Yeah, who knew he even snacked? It just goes to show you that he's a regular guy just like us and puts his pants on one leg at a time. Unless he's sitting down, of course.

"Yeah, well," I said philosophically, "you get what you get and you don't get upset." That was one Mrs. Lehman taught us in kindergarten. Still true today.

Marcus shot me a look that seemed to say he thought I was kind of being a moron, and suddenly I regretted saying anything.

He immediately shoved his arm into the small gap between the snack machine and the pop machine and reached around in back. It was a struggle, since he couldn't see what he was doing.

"Hit your buttons," he told me, and as soon as I figured out that he meant for me to make my snack selection, I did. "And keep holding them down."

Suddenly, the big device shook and all the lights went out. When they came back on, the vending machine seemed to take a minute to figure out what was going on, then one of the big screws inside started turning and it dropped the requested package of Chile Picante CornNuts into the slot.

"That wouldn't work on one of the new machines," Volger explained, "but this one is an old friend."

And, before you say anything, the answer is NO, I *don't* consider 1.4 ounces of corn, partially hydrogenated soybean oil, salt, and maltodextrin to be appropriate nutrition for a growing boy, but survival sometimes means making do with the resources at hand.

Then I had another thought. "It never took my dollar."

"I appreciate your honesty, Tommy," Marcus said. "But let me ask you this: How many times have you inserted money into a vending machine and *not* gotten the right change, if any? This just evens things out. Besides, just you carrying around that package of CornNuts is like free advertising for Kraft Foods, which is worth way more than the chump change you *tried* to give them and they wouldn't take anyway."

Marcus has a great way of putting everything into perspective. And, man, as soon as he saw I had a problem, he stepped in with a solution.

"Tommy," he said, sighing like a dude with something on his mind, "I'm glad I ran into you. I've got a little problem, and maybe you can help me with it."

I have to admit that I was flattered. It's gratifying to have a reputation as a problem solver.

"Look," Marcus continued, "I hesitate to bring it up, because it's about your new buddy."

"Griff?!" I immediately knew where he was going with this. "Carver is *not* my buddy, at all!"

"Really?" he said. "I gotta tell you, Tommy. That's kind of a relief. I'm not so sure about that guy."

"Well, I'm sure!" I told him. "I'm sure he's dirty. He was kicked out of his last school for who knows what, and he let this class skipper go after he caught him, and I overheard—"

I was about to say I knew about his vague threats to Volger from under the cafeteria table but decided against it. Marcus might not like the idea of my electronic eavesdropping, even if it's in the service of the greater good. People can be touchy about that stuff. I quickly steered the conversation to safer waters.

"Look, I even talked to Verity about him," I explained. "She says we can nail this guy to the wall as soon as I can get enough evidence to expose him in the *Liberty Bell*."

Marcus was quiet for a minute, and I could tell he was thinking.

"You know what, Tommy . . ." he started. But then he waved off the idea. "Oh, it's none of my business. I'm sure you know what you're doing. You're a Hall Monitor and I'm just some guy."

"No, no," I told him, not wanting him to feel inferior. "You're one smart, together dude. I'd love to hear what you think."

"I'm sure whatever you want to do is fine," Marcus told me. "I just wondered if trying him in the press, publicly like that, is the right thing to do. I mean, he is a brother officer and everything, right?"

"I guess . . ." I said, kind of uncomfortably.

"Verity's cool and everything, but she's only worried about her byline in the *Bell*. And besides," Marcus continued, "you would really need some rock-solid proof to put in print, and how likely is it that Carver is going to hand that to you on a silver cafeteria tray? You might be waiting a long time for that. Maybe forever."

"What else can I do?" I wondered.

Marcus seemed to give this some thought. "What's that

fat kid's name? Your captain."

"Delane?" I ventured. Then I set him straight about the "fat" comment, explaining that you are merely husky, burly even.

"Yeah, Delane." Marcus nodded. "You should go to him with this. Tell him everything you know. Your suspicions, gut feeling, anything. Make sure he knows any shady thing Carver's been up to."

"Well, how is that any better than the newspaper?"

"Because Delane can act immediately, without you waiting around for some evidence that might never come," Marcus explained. "Especially with the principal breathing down his neck. You know how Sprague is about this stuff, terrified he's going to lose his job if the school bus tires aren't properly inflated. You might even start by dropping him an anonymous note."

I wasn't so sure about Marcus's suggestion. Verity's usually pretty smart about these things. Besides, there was the article to consider.

"How would you feel," Marcus continued, "if Carver got caught doing something heinous while he's still in Safety Patrol? It would besmirch the entire force and all because you failed to act immediately."

I nodded, making a mental note to Google *besmirch*.

"Jeez, would you listen to me yack?" Marcus laughed.

"Just like a politician, huh? Look, I'm sure whatever you figure out will be great. I'm just happy to have a friend like you I can unload on. Thanks, man."

I finished off the bag of CornNuts and watched him vanish into the traffic of students. He was right, of course. I should've come to you with my suspicions immediately, Delane. I regret not doing so. And I hope you appreciate that it takes a Big Man to admit his mistakes.

Leave it to Marcus Volger to put me back on the right path.

CHAPTER EIGHT

HELEN NUTTING
GUIDANCE COUNSELOR
RAMPART MIDDLE SCHOOL

Continuation of the RECORDED INTERVIEW with seventh grader Griffin Carver.

GRIFF: "Rise and shine!" That was the Old Lady. No surprise there.

"I'll rise, but I won't shine," I answered. It wasn't really a response, it was a ritual. I pulled a shirt out of the laundry pile and gave the armpit the sniff test. Musty, but not too ripe for school.

As I woke up, the weight of the murky depths of Rampart Middle settled on my shoulders again and I had an overwhelming desire to crawl back under the covers for another year or two.

Instead, I headed for the can and I splashed some cold water across my freckles and pulled it together some, then got an eyeful of myself in the mirror. Is that what I looked like now? Twelve. Man, eleven feels like a lifetime ago.

"I'm getting too old for this junk," I said aloud to no one, shaking my head. Then I slipped the rolled-up red belt into my pocket and I was myself again.

Like always, I passed the Creature's door on my way down the hall. It was covered in bumper stickers and pictures of rock bands I'd never heard of and topped off with a chunk of traffic barricade including the warning light, which was always flashing. City property. The Creature was a regular collage artist. I heard the music start up and took off down the stairs.

The cereal bowl was waiting for me. So were the questions.

"How did band practice go yesterday?" asked the Old Lady.

"Band practice never goes well this early in the year," I answered without hesitating.

It wasn't exactly a lie. I never lie. I equivocate. I answer questions with questions. I'm vague. But I don't lie.

In my experience an outright lie is a death trap you set for yourself. It starts out as a tiny thread, but you have to keep weaving more and more supports for that first strand until it becomes a huge, inescapable web. And in my line of work, I can't afford to be trapped.

But I was certainly misleading the Old Lady and, necessary or not, it made my Golden Os sit in my gut like a pile of sharp-cornered Legos.

She let it go at that. I was lucky. If her radar was on, she wouldn't let up. Everything I know about interrogation, I learned from her.

"Griffin," she said tentatively, "I know you must be disappointed about not doing patrol this year—"

"I'm not," I answered, trying to nip this in the bud.

"It's just . . . well, you know what it did to your brother."

I HAVE NO BROTHER.

That's what I wanted to shout. But I didn't.

Best thing I could do was get out of there. And fast.

With the new school allure now scraped off of Rampart, the Old Lady no longer insisted on dropping me off. Like some disaster was more likely to occur on day one than on day thirty-two. Mom logic. Go figure.

I headed out to the wheels. My bike is a Marley Carson, a knockoff Schwinn manufactured in Micronesia (which is a real place, by the way . . . I hear *Micro-nesia* and I immediately think it's a comic book world where everyone is tiny). Anyway, the Marley may not be pretty to look at, but I've done a few mods on it over the years and, underneath the deceptive rust patches and partially peeled-off stickers promoting canceled cartoons, she's a gearhead's dream. I also added some pretty spectacular aftermarket items across the handlebars, which I keep under wraps, hidden by a long-unused paperboy sack. Rollers. Siren. I even have a PA system. Sometimes a loud noise or flashing lights is all it takes to shock a kid back into socially acceptable behavior.

Other times . . . well, let's just say that sometimes you've gotta lean on the pedals. Fortunately, the Marley delivers. I can't tell you how many glittery, hot rod flame-covered crotch rockets I've dusted. They never saw it comin'.

These incidents were, of course, in the line of duty. For the most part.

I rolled onto campus and automatically went into assessment mode. Near the baseball backstop there was some interaction between a Neanderthal with some un-diagnosed glandular problem receiving papers out of a brainoid superachiever who looked like he was about eight. Coercion? Homework for hire? Impossible to tell from this distance and, yes, everything in me wanted to aim my Marley Carson in that direction and find out. But that would blow everything. So I just rolled by.

Two minutes later, my ride was locked (at the end of the bike racks, for immediate access) and I was walking into the school with the usual pack of stragglers when I caught Verity's eye. She looked at me in a weird way, half concerned, half confused.

"Hey, Fourth Estate," I called to her, "what's news?"

Wasn't sure if I was going to get a tart comment. Then I saw her jaw tighten and she looked the other way. For all her attitude, Verity's a true-blue goody-goody and news travels fast even in a school this size.

Poor Verity. Don't get me wrong. She's great, obviously. But she is very by the book. Maybe even more than Tommy, in her own way. Journalists don't think outside the box, because the box has their byline written on it, right under the big block-letter headline.

"Griff!" This was Delane, calling after me. His voice echoed down the hallway despite the throng of students. I turned and he looked at the floor awkwardly just before he pulled it together.

"My office," he barked. "Now!"

Delane must be taking speech classes, because the mean voice was working. I got a cold chill, if just for a second. Then I shrugged it off, of course.

"Don't look so worried, man," I told him as I passed him and entered the Multipurpose Room. "It's not like this is the first time I've ever been in trouble with my CO."

"No," he answered me, his voice heavy and serious, "but it is the last." It was quite a delivery. Maybe he was in Drama Club to boot.

The Multipurpose Room was full of off-duty peace officers. I didn't know the squad yet, of course, but all the usual types were there. The husky kid looking for friends. The joker. Tough girl with something to prove. Meat, Reams, and Ciardi. There was also a set of twins who I mentally named Good Cop/Bad Cop. They stopped talking and gave me the stink eye. Nothing too strange about that. Standard new-guy scenario.

Or was it? Was something else going on here? Something more than met the stink eye?

Delane ushered me into his office, which was really a converted broom closet. Still, not bad. Most COs didn't even rate that. Maybe Delane was more resourceful than just the transcript packer I'd originally sussed him up as. He'd done the place up like a real office. Desk, flags (U.S., state, and school), Ionic Breeze fan.

"So, Griffin Carver," I hear a voice say, "we meet again."

The swivel chair behind Delane's tiny desk spun around and there Sprangue sat in all his glory. I didn't give him the satisfaction of looking surprised.

"Ah, Principal . . . uh, Sprangue, right?" I added the stumble on his name. It's important to remind our elected officials that the world doesn't revolve around them. "So, what brings the big man down here with the plebes?"

"You do, Carver," he said, sizing me up. "Let's just say a little bird told me that—"

"Seriously?" I interrupted. "You're going to lead with 'a little bird told you'? You really kick it old school." I figured I was already on his naughty list. Might as well get the shots in while I could.

"Sit down," he snapped. It was an order, not a request. He must've forgotten that we weren't in his office.

"We're in a supply closet," I helpfully reminded him. "If I sit down, I'll be outside."

"I don't usually interfere with the affairs of the student associations, but I received an anonymous note informing me that I might have a troublemaker on my hands."

"Obviously, you do," I noted. "Troublemakers are always sending anonymous notes."

"Imagine my surprise," he said, ignoring me, "when I discovered the note was referring to *you*." Surprise? He probably danced a jig on his desk.

He'd had enough of our snappy exchange—I could tell by the way he snatched up the manila folder on the desk. My old captain used to call them vanilla folders, and I never let him live that down.

"I had your permanent record sent up from St. Finbar's, Carver," he explained. They always start that way. Must be in the principal playbook.

They make a big deal over that permanent record. How permanent is it, really? What if society falls apart and we're reduced to living like post-apocalyptic cavemen? What if international hackers destroy the world data-base? How long will those non-acid-free paper copies of my so-called permanent record last, anyway? Forever? I don't think so.

"Lot of interesting reading material here," Sprangue continued, leafing through the file, pretending to read it. This guy is exactly what you'd expect. Not smart enough to be a real teacher but slick enough to sweet-talk the school board into giving him a cake job where he can do what he does best: lord it over anyone and everyone. His job goal: Keep this sweet gig, whatever it takes.

"It says here you frisked the school superintendent?" It wasn't really a question. He was smiling. Like a tiger.

It was true about the superintendent. But I had probable cause. I mean, why was she so vehement about going around the metal detectors? You'd think that the fact that she had a pretty serious set of nail clippers stashed in her purse would vindicate me, but no. I'm telling you, no airline on earth would let her on board with that thing.

But I didn't tell Sprangue that.

"And you evacuated the cafeteria during the Booster Club's bake sale?" he went on.

"The cookies were made with peanut oil," I said. It wasn't an excuse. I just got tired of hearing his voice, so I thought I'd volunteer my side. "We had three students with allergies so severe that just one whiff of those peanuts would send them into anaphylactic—"

"You're a troublemaker, Carver!" he shouted, interrupting me. A real politician. I bet he never interrupts the school board. "And I hate troublemakers."

Translation: He doesn't like it when people make waves. Even if it'd take a tsunami to wash this place clean.

"And I won't jeopardize Rampart's spotless reputation for . . ." He kept going on and, yeah, I'll admit it, it got to me. I lost my cool.

"With all due respect, Principal!" I interrupted, perhaps a little louder than necesary. "A reputation isn't the same thing as the truth. This place has more skeletons in the closet than *Zombie Palace 4*! Under the happy facade here, corruption lurks. It's my duty to—"

"Delane," interrupted Sprangue. "Show him."

I could tell Delane was not too excited about the prospect, but he obeyed, calling up a series of digital photos on his laptop. They were all close-ups of the floor. That ancient Rampart Middle linoleum.

"Notice the scuff marks." Sprangue grinned. "Consistent with running. They weren't there before your shift last Tuesday. You're aware of our no-running policy. Anything you care to tell me?"

Yeah, not likely.

"I know how it is, Griff," he baited me. "Some kid gets out of line. What choice do you have but to chase him down? Right?"

It was a simple interrogation technique. The Old Lady could run rings around this guy. I clammed up. The principal gave Delane the nod.

"At approximately 9:47 a.m.," Delane read, "substitute teacher Marion Sood saw what she described as 'a blur of motion' followed by the sound of 'running feet.'

"Maybe somebody takes off," he went on. "You and your partner get caught up in the moment and—"

"No," I bit. "Just me. Rodriguez didn't run. Whatever reprimand you have to dish out is just for me to take—"

"Reprimand?" Sprague grinned again. His smile

broke through his mask of shocked disapproval. "I don't know how they did things at your old school, but let me assure you . . . here at Rampart Middle, we operate under the rule of law."

He was happy. Too happy just to be handing me a pink slip.

"And I'm guy who puts the *zero* in zero tolerance."

My mind was racing. What was he up to?

"If you think you're getting a slap on the wrist here, Carver, think again."

He wasn't going to expel me. Or even suspend me. Not for that kind of infraction. So what was the middle ground? What was between detention and expulsion? What was he . . . ?

No. He couldn't.

"Know what a loose cannon is, Carver?" he asked. "In the old days of war at sea, those big cannons had to be lashed to the deck. A loose cannon would roll around, smashing everything in its path. Maybe even punch a hole in the hull and sink the whole ship. There's no room in *this* school's Safety Patrol for a loose cannon, kid."

"Principal Sprangue, you can't—"

"You're a loose cannon, Griff," he said. Sounded like he was passing a sentence. A death sentence. He made eye contact with Delane. His cue.

"Griffin Carver," said Delane, his official tone reverberating in my head like he was shouting to me from the depths of a bottomless storm drain. "Consider this your official notification that you are hereby relieved of duty and removed from the roster of active Hall Monitors."

I said something. Maybe "what?" or "no!" I don't really know. It's like a half-remembered dream now. The kind of dream you have after a parent-free evening of Heath Bar Crunch and the Horror Channel. The principal broke the spell.

"His badge," Sprangue said.

I didn't seem to understand.

"I'm afraid I have to ask you to . . . surrender your badge," Delane said to the floor.

I couldn't move. Not sure for how long. But long enough for Delane to have to talk again.

"Don't make this any harder, Griff."

I had to command my body to move like it was a remote-controlled car. It moved like it needed new batteries. But it moved.

The badge stuck on the belt momentarily, like it didn't want to come off. So much for dignity. I yanked and it gave.

I tossed it onto the desk. The belt followed it. My

property, but that was a technicality. What was I supposed to do with it? Frame it?

"Well, Carver." Sprangue grimaced. "How does it feel to be just a regular—"

"Principal Sprangue!" Delane almost shouted. Then, reeling his sympathy in, "Bell's going to ring any second. I really need to get to class."

Even in my fog I knew he'd taken a big chance for me. I didn't waste it. Before Sprangue could open his mouth again, I was out of that broom closet.

Then I had to pass through the squad room. No easy feat. Through the moisture that was accumulating in the corners of my eyes despite my best efforts, I could just make out the distorted faces of my fellow officers.

Former fellow officers.

A whole set of unlearned nicknames and inside jokes fell away from me like a spent rocket stage, ready to burn up in the atmosphere. The stink eye they'd glared at me earlier took on new meaning. I'd glared it myself at disgraced Hall Monitors. I'd know better now.

It was hard to make out their faces through the suspended waterfall, but I did see one.

Tommy.

He tried to look away but couldn't.

I reached into my pocket.

"You dropped this," I said.

I flipped it to him and stepped out into the hall, into the great unwashed. Didn't hear it hit the floor, so he must've caught it.

Probably happy to see it. Those Spy Bling coins don't grow on trees.

CHAPTER NINE

~~Dear Diary,~~

~~Hey, Diary—~~

~~What up, D.?~~

Hello, Journal.

There, I feel better already. Just changing your name to Journal has kept you out of the recycler for another twenty-four. Consider yourself fortunate that my hard drive is smoking and I just reached the last page of my coil-top-lock wire-bound spiral notebook (perforated for easy tear-out). You're still on death row, but you've had a reprieve. And covering your fluorescent pinkness with black Sharpie ink might prolong your use even further.

Anyway, I need to get this all down while it's still fresh, so you are elected.

Like most things worth reporting, it started with a combination of the typical and the unusual. First, the phone rang. Typical. Then I picked up. Unusual. I never pick up the phone when I'm at home. It's either a refinancing robot or someone who doesn't talk to me. If the Apathetic Five need to ask me something about a story, they know to IM me. That way they can't hear the sarcasm in my voice when I tell them something encouraging. But this time, maybe because my laptop was behind a Genius Bar somewhere and I was on wireless withdrawal, I picked up.

I heard Tiffany's voice on the other end and told her I'd bellow for my sister.

"Actually?" she said. "I called to talk to you?"

Just so you know, everything Tiffany says sounds like a question, but I'll turn some of those question marks into periods so I don't go insane when I read this later. She hadn't tried to talk to me since the unfortunate incident in June when she attempted to highlight my hair. I was actually curious.

"I'm at the Palace," she said.

From the explosions, bells, and kid noise, I'd pretty much already assumed she was calling from work.

Tiffany means the snack bar at the Magical Palace Family Fun and Goony Golf Center. That's where she is when she isn't sleeping, doing her nails in class, or at a party with the Blond Amigos, a group that includes my sister, who, like Tiffany, is not blond. In fact, only two of the members are even in the ballpark. The name was a holdover from an earlier incarnation of the group.

"There's a kid here from your school," she told me. "He's got a Rampart Middle backpack."

"Okay," I said. Thanks for the update, Tif.

"Yeah, you should come and get him," she said cryptically. "He's freaking out."

I didn't know what she was talking about and told her so.

"I think Jerome—he's the assistant manager—is going to call security," she said by way of explanation.

"Tiffany, I still don't see what this has to do with—"

"This kid?" She cut me off. "I call him Shooter? Because he only plays the shooting games? He's nice. I don't want him to get into trouble. So why don't you come here and take him home or something."

"Maybe," I said, hopefully not sounding too condescending, "you should call his parents."

"Yeah, I don't want to get him in trouble?" she told me. "And also, I don't know his last name, so I can't call them anyway. I think his real first name is Gritt or Biff or something weird."

"Griff?!" I blurted out.

"Yeah," she said. "Maybe. Probably."

One quick phone call of my own later, I was out the door.

I didn't really need to take the bus, but it pulled up right when I was passing the bus stop nearest my house. Ten minutes later I was walking over the non-functioning drawbridge that spanned a shallow moat of stagnant dyed-blue water. Magical!

I've been to more than my share of parties at the Ye Olde Magical Palace Family Fun and Goony Golf Center, but I'm never quite prepared for the assault of noise, lights, and rancid oil smell from the deep-fat fryer that meets you at the plaster of paris arched gateway.

I was just passing the line of Skee-Ball alleys when I saw Tiffany wave at me from the snack area. This was the most proactive I've ever seen her, which isn't saying much, but I hurried over to her anyway.

"Shooter's usually really nice," she said to me immediately instead of "hello" or "thanks for getting here so quickly." "But not tonight. He's all 'roid raged out."

"This thing is broken!" a voice yelled above the clamor of a hundred arcade games.

Using the convex fish-eye mirror mounted to the ceiling, I looked down an aisle of flashing and shrieking video games and saw him pointing at Maginot Line, one of the least popular, according to Tiffany, first-person shooters. There was no mistake. It was Griff, all right.

"The sights are way off and the action is bad and I nailed about two dozen Krauts that aren't registering!" Griff shouted to no one in particular.

When I say it was Griff, I mean it looked like him, but it was like it wasn't him at all. All his cool was gone. I know, not much of a diagnosis, but that was what it seemed like. It was as if his body had been possessed by some hyperactive kid who'd forgotten to take his medication.

"He's not usually like this," Tiffany told me, so concerned she could barely apply the top coat to her pinkie nail. She said "Shooter" was different from the noisy, jostling middle schoolers who came in. He didn't brag or strut. He didn't even enter his initials when he got top score. He seemed to be playing against himself. Shooter was serious. He treated his arcade time like it was a job. More than Tiffany did, anyway.

"Sir, the Magical Palace has strict guidelines regarding the raising of voices." This was Jerome, the assistant manager Tiffany had mentioned on the phone. Tiffany didn't need to tell me. He had the looks of a teenage boy who'd read the Magical Palace handbook cover to cover.

Tiffany hasn't read the handbook, of course. Working concession in her heinous medieval serf outfit was already more than any rational person would expect of her for minimum wage.

The crazy Griff impersonator didn't seem overly concerned with the prohibition on voice-raising at the Magical Palace. He was really getting into it with Jerome. Yelling. The game wasn't just broken, it was "fixed." The Magic Palace was clearly illegally squeezing its clientele for everything they could, one token at a time.

Griff was really raving now. Come to think of it, he didn't think anyone here had the intelligence to rig a sophisticated shoot-'em-up (or "shmup") to kill the player off early. The Palace must be part of some vast, corrupt family fun center conspiracy, exchanging high-tech gimmicking of the games in exchange for "protection" and, of course, the lion's share of ill-gotten pickings.

At that very moment I saw Tommy walking by the giant fiberglass fake winches that were designed to look like they hoisted up the drawbridge but were really trash cans.

Griff would've seen him if he hadn't been busy raving at the assistant manager. I darted behind Griff, grabbed Tommy by the arm, and circled back to Tiffany's snack bar dragging him behind me.

"I'm sorry, sir," said Jerome, who was clearly required to call the patrons "sir" or "miss" despite the fact that, even at his diminutive size, he could, generally speaking, toss them over his undernourished shoulder. "But one more outburst and I'm going to have to require you to leave the premises. We don't want any trouble here."

"Well, you GOT trouble, pal!" Griff screamed, drawing every eye in the place.

The volume of his own voice and the gaping stares of a couple dozen kids were enough to shock Griff back into a semblance of self-control. He mumbled something like an apology to Jerome and skulked away from him and from the reproachful eyes of Klaw Krane addicts and redemption gamers.

And headed right for Tiffany's counter! I pulled Tommy down to the floor and covered his mouth before he could say anything. Right above us, Griff plunked his extra-jumbo drink container down. It made a loud, exaggerated TOK sound.

"Large Coke," he said. "Easy on that ice lever."

"Sorry, kid," Tiffany started. "No refills."

"I'm not asking for a freebie," Griff said, his voice starting to rise. "I'm just ordering another Coke."

From beneath the counter, we watched as Tiffany went to the soda dispenser and filled a large cup. She plopped it down in front of Griff, who ripped open a new straw, plunged it through the plastic to-go lid, and sucked up the beverage greedily.

A sour look crossed his face. "What's the big idea?! This is soda water! You left the Coke out of my Coke!"

"It's on the house," Tiffany said.

"I don't want free bubbly water," he growled, "I want what I ordered!"

"You've had enough sugar and caffeine for one day, kid," Tiffany told him. She'd cut off enough middle schoolers to know this went down one of two ways. But Griff wasn't about to break out the sob story. Not even on a soda rampage.

He started emptying his pockets, and I could hear the change hit the counter. A purple string of prize tickets landed on the floor right next to Tommy. Evidently, this day even had Shooter straying into Skee-Ball territory.

"I can pay!" Griff barked. "See? All I want is another Coke!"

"Your money's no good here, Shooter," Tiffany said flatly. I don't think she'd meant to use her nickname for him.

"I SAID GIMME A COKE!"

This was a real shout. Every eye in the place was on him for a moment, and in a place where kids are paying real money for the privilege of keeping their eyes glued to a game screen, that's really saying something. I looked up at the security mirror and saw Jerome put down his Dustpan Pro and make his way toward the bar, ready for a kick out.

"Don't make this ugly, kid," Tiffany pleaded. But she couldn't see any other way this could play out. Tommy looked at me, still totally confused, not knowing what he was supposed to do. I gestured for him to stay put.

"Griff!" a woman's voice called.

Griff looked up, and some of the rage and confusion melted from his face. Even though the ceiling mirror made everything in it look tiny, I could see self-awareness was seeping back into Griff's brain from the corners of his skull. He was coming to his senses. And he couldn't have been very happy about the situation he was finding himself in.

The woman rushed over to him and knelt down, quickly assessing his physical condition. Although Mr. Button would chafe at my making unconfirmed assumptions, she was clearly Griff's mom, but unlike my mom, she didn't automatically go for the hysterics. First, she gave him a once-over, a quick examination like a paramedic. All limbs intact, no broken bones, no swelling. Who knows, maybe she worked in an ER.

"I've been looking for you in every arcade in town," said Mrs. Carver, roughly wrestling him into a jacket. Noting the mildness of the early evening, I couldn't help thinking that the dressing was more of a power play.

"I was right here," replied Griff, clinging to some tiny vestige of attitude. The woman let it pass and then, putting the pieces together, she glanced up at the counter and saw the extra-jumbo cup. Her eyes flashed with understanding and trained directly onto Tiffany like a cobra's.

"How many of these did you give him?" Mrs. Carver asked accusingly.

Tiffany later told me she'd served him at least five.

"I dunno," Tiffany said flatly. But she could tell from Mrs. Carver's face that she wasn't buying it.

"How many?" she repeated. "Or do I need to call the manager?"

Mrs. Carver's challenge just hung in the air for a moment.

"How should I know?" Tiffany said. "All these brats look the same to me. I just work here, lady."

I have to admit that I was impressed. I always thought Tiffany was the most useless of the Blond Amigos, which is really saying something. But evidently, there's a little bit of steel under all that makeup and hair spray.

In the mirror I saw Griff's mom shoot Tiffany "the look,"

but she was clearly posturing. It's no secret that the Mom Look is only effective on the actual children, biological or otherwise, of the mother.

Nevertheless, she kept her eyes on Tiffany as she grabbed Griff by the wrist and announced to no one in particular, "We're going."

For a moment I was afraid that Tiffany was going to close with the company mandated "Thanks for making the Magical Palace your home away from home," but she knew better.

She threw away the boy's cup and dropped the straw and lid into the recycle bin that had a sticker on it that said GREEN IS MAGICAL! Then Tiffany gave the counter a wipe down and said, "They're gone."

As we climbed to our feet, I could tell Tommy was stunned. Anyone would be. It was a highly charged emotional scene.

"Is that what you called me down here to see?" he asked accusingly. "Why? What was the big idea?"

The real reason probably had something to do with Tommy going to Delane with the story instead of coming to me. But seeing Griff like that was even more dramatic than I'd imagined when Tiffany called me.

"You needed to see that before I asked you a question," I told him.

"What?" he asked.

"*Theoretically*," I began, "would you say Griff's reaction to getting booted off Safety Patrol is what you might expect from a tough, hardened criminal who was looking out for himself?"

I hadn't seen Tommy think so hard since . . . well, ever. I couldn't help pushing him a little farther.

"Well? Is it?"

CHAPTER TEN

RAMPART MIDDLE SCHOOL SAFETY PATROL
Incident Report

TO:
Delane Owens, Divisional CO

FROM:
Thomas Rodriguez, HP 2nd Class

DATE:
Friday, September 25, 3:18 p.m.

INCIDENT:
Where Do I Begin?

Delane, if you are reading this, and it only stands to reason that you are, one of two things has happened. Either somehow everything has turned out fine. Or, more likely, everything has gone very, very badly and you're trying to make some sense of everything.

As you've probably come to expect from me, I have thought ahead and am prepared. I have given this IR to Guidance Councelor Nutting, with instructions that if anything should happen to me, this report should be safely delivered into your hands.

As you know, the last time we talked, I reported to you my suspicions about Hall Monitor Carver. Based on his behavior and, I'm ashamed to admit this, hearsay, I just couldn't believe that Griff was anything less than 100 percent guilty.

Anyone would think so. He was kicked out of his old school! Okay, maybe the charges were dropped and the records were sealed, but whatever went down back at his old school was weird.

Then for various reasons that I won't go into now, Verity showed me several articles she dug up on Griff, which you'll find attached.

TWEEN HERO TAMES INTERSECTION

In recent weeks, local pedestrians find themselves

collectively breathing a sigh of relief, and it's all thanks to a local lawman... who has a paper route! The intersection of Maple Avenue and Third Streets has long been infamous as a gathering place for rowdy grade schoolers, a corner to be avoided by senior citizens, young mothers and anyone who values peace and quiet, but a six year-old crossing guard has changed all that . . .

LOCAL BOY HAS SAFETY IN HIS 'CORNER'

At the annual Safety Awards Dinner held at the Morris Center Friday night, one concerned citizen walked away with more trophies than anyone else. Third grader Griffin Carver may have been the youngest recipient, but he certainly made an impression as he walked to the stage again and again to receive . . .

CROSSING GUARD RISKS ALL TO SAVE KITTENS

A grateful mother tabby purred joyfully yesterday as she was reunited with her wayward litter of meowing kitties. The heroic actions of a young safety patrol officer who races across a busy thoroughfare to . . .

COURAGEOUS CORNER COP PUTS KIBBOSH
ON MOTORCROSS MENACE

I have news for those jaded cynics who believe there
are no more heroes. There are still individuals among us
willing to stand up for what's right, even in the face of
overwhelming odds. Case in point, Griffin Carver. Griff,
as he likes to be called, is a fifth grader at St. Finbar's
who . . .

Pretty strong stuff, right? Well, these articles got me
thinking: How does a righteous dude just 180° like that?

That question kept gnawing away at me. Even when I
turned in that night, I couldn't stop thinking about it. The
Scout manual recommends a minimum of seven hours
of sleep. Ten hours is optimum during these years of
accelerated growth. Based on my sleep patterns, I think it
likely that I'm entering another growth spurt now.

Anyway, I got maybe . . . six? hours that night.

That was no good for anybody. I had to do something
about it.

I was on hall duty this morning, between second and
third periods. And, as you know, that's a pretty hairy watch,
not a cakewalk full of groggy kids like first shift, but nothing
I can't handle. I was temporarily partnered with Dugan and,
brotherhood of officers aside, that's kind of like not being

partnered at all.

But, like I said, nothing I couldn't handle. I was still brooding about this whole Griff thing when I saw Marcus down the hall, campaigning as usual, with the usual crowd, Ben Gave, Morgan Boca, and the rest of them.

"Dugan," I said, "why don't you check the expiration dates on the fire extinguishers in the west corridor?"

"But we just did that last week," he whined at me.

"You're absolutely sure it was last week?" I asked. "Not the week before? You're *sure*, now?" I knew Dugan's short-term memory (like his long-term memory) was not the most reliable. And I knew he knew that too. I saw his forehead pucker and knew he was thinking.

"I'm not *one hundred percent* sure," he admitted.

If I didn't know better, I'd swear Dugan mumbled something under his breath as he headed west down the main hallway. I don't know what's getting into these new recruits. Back when I was a rookie, we obeyed orders without—but I digest.

I didn't really care about the fire extinguishers. I mean, I always care about school safety, but I knew the equipment was in good working order. It was a ruse. I needed to talk to someone . . . alone.

"Heeeeey, Tommy!" said Marcus, as friendly as ever.

"Marcus, have you got a minute?" I asked him.

"I always have time for my friends." He smiled at me. Just for a second I thought, Are we really friends? He always says I'm his friend, but it isn't like we hang out or anything. He's never been over to my house or asked me to play Xbox or whatever. But then I thought, He's probably just busy. I mean, everybody knows what a great guy Marcus is. I thought about dropping the whole thing, but I'd already interrupted him when he was shaking hands, and I couldn't think of anything else to say, so I just pushed on.

"It's about Griff Carver," I said.

The smile vanished from his face for a moment. Seriously, that happy grin that's always there, gone. He glanced over at Ben and Morgan but didn't say anything. It was like he was a totally different guy. Then he turned to me and the smile was back. I thought maybe I'd imagined the whole thing.

"Stay away from that kid, Tommy," Marcus suggested, full of concern. "You did right to report him. Griff's trouble."

"I so get what you're saying," I responded, "but he's actually pretty cool sometimes. He just got this messed-up idea that you were, I don't know, some kind of bad guy . . ."

"I told you," he said, still smiling, but with a different

115

kind of smile, "he's trouble. And he's going to get you in trouble too if you're not careful. Understand?"

"Look, I set him straight," I explained. "Told him you weren't a criminal operator or whatever crazy idea he got stuck in his—"

Marcus Volger pushed me against the marble wall by the broken drinking fountain. Not so hard as to make a scene, you understand. Maybe he was just making a point and got carried away.

"Tommy," he said, in a way I'd never heard him speak before, "election's tomorrow. I don't have time for this right now. And you need to keep your mouth shut. People could overhear you and misunderstand something you're saying. Get it?"

Of course. The school election. He was probably under a lot of pressure right now. I hadn't thought. Still . . .

"If you could just talk to Sprangue about Griff," I said. "Tell him that it was all a misunderstanding and that—"

He grabbed my face. Seriously! He grabbed my face like my older brother sometimes does to get me to stop talking. Nobody in the hall could see, because Volger's friends were right behind him, blocking the view. "Carver even *thinking* about causing trouble for me is enough reason to neutralize him.

"Like I said," he continued, grinning. "I don't have time

to explain it to you right now. Elections. But my friends here have time. They'll explain for me."

Suddenly, Marcus, the lockers, and the wall were getting smaller. I realized that Ben and Morgan had me by the arms and were dragging me . . .

The funny thing is that it sounds just like a jet engine. I know that because my Camp Scout troop visited Metro Airport and were given an up-close and personal look at a Learjet 45, and I can say with some confidence that its rear-mounted engine sounds exactly like the flush of Toilet #3 in the Main Hall boys' lavatory.

But only if you are listening from *inside* the toilet.

Which I was, thanks to Big Ben and Morgan Boca, who clearly have considerable experience administering a regulation swirly. It's a common enough crime. In the United Kingdom, it's known as bogwashing. If you were to experience this in Australia, where flushed water swirls counterclockwise, you would have received a *dunny-flushing*.

I struggled, of course, but it was mostly reflex. From my training, I know there's no escape from this maneuver when it is being properly executed. And, from where I was sitting, it clearly was.

But I'll tell you, Delane, much more than the physical

117

discomfort, the pain I felt was from embarrassment. No, not from the humiliation of the prank, but from my own blindness. That gushing torrent of toilet water splashing me in the face was a wake-up call.

I had no idea this kind of activity was occurring. On *my* beat. Mine! But if this was happening to me (and, believe me, it was), it was happening to other kids too. Right under my nose.

In that moment it became quite obvious to me that the Rampart Middle I thought I knew so well was nothing more than an illusion. In all my time here, I'd been looking only at the surface. The nice, shiny, multiple Certificate of Excellence in State Education award-winning exterior. But there's another side. A Dark Side.

It exists in the same place as the school we know and love at the same time. But, unless you know what to look for, it's invisible.

You know that look Griff gets in his eyes? Like he's squinting? And how he doesn't look right at you while you're talking to him? I think maybe it's because he's searching for the Dark Side.

And from now on, now that I know it's there, I'll be looking for it too.

At least, that's what I was thinking in those few seconds (it felt like hours) that Volger's buddies held my head down in the toilet bowl.

The next thing I knew, I was alone and drying my hair with the wall-mounted air blower. I only used a few paper towels. Why should the environment suffer just because I was the victim of aggravated mischief?

Of course, duty dictated my next move, and, before my hair was even dry, I was marching to your office to make my report. Reams and Montelongo were instantly on their feet when they saw me heading toward your door unannounced.

"He's busy," Montelongo quickly piped in as I brushed by him. A lot of the hall cops talk about how big Roy Montelongo is, but you won't be surprised that he doesn't intimidate me in the least. I opened your door and stepped in.

"You better be sitting down, chief," I told you, "because I got some two-Twinkie news for you."

You slowly looked up at me with the "you *didn't* just walk in here" look on your face that I expected. Then, the voice.

"Sounds like some pretty earth-shattering information," he said. Volger said, I mean. Now, as my eyes adjusted to your office, I could see him. His smile was on but somehow looked different to me now. Like the grin on the face of Mrs. Dochterman's pit bull just before he sank his teeth into my calf.

The world started spinning around me faster than the

water in Toilet #3. I couldn't tell you my story with Volger there! You know how smooth he is. He'd just laugh it off. I'd sound crazy.

Then, I'm ashamed to say, an even worse thought popped into my head. What if Volger wasn't there? Would it be safe to talk then? Maybe not!! What if you were in on it? What if you, Delane, were somehow part of Volger's crew?

I know, that would be nuts, right? As the head of Safety Patrol, your office embodies justice and right! Maybe so, but fifteen minutes earlier I wouldn't have thought the great Marcus Volger capable of snapping his fingers and initiating a swirling!

It was like I'd stepped into another dimension. The kind of dimension where everyone looks pretty much the same, I mean, maybe they have a goatee or something, but the big difference is that they are totally evil!

So help me, Delane, in that moment, I didn't know if I could trust you.

"Well?" you asked me, somewhat impatiently. "What is it, Tommy?" I wasn't sure how long it took me to think all this stuff. You'd know better than me. I closed my mouth. Had to think fast.

"Did you write down Mr. Cogan's math assignment?" I improvised coolly.

"I don't have Mr. Cogan for math," you barked at me,

looking at me like I was nuts. "Tommy, we're not even in the same grade!"

"Oh, yeah." I nodded, still in character. "That's right. Never mind." Okay, that was not my smoothest cover, but I was under a lot of stress.

My heart still reverberating like a dual-shock controller, I sauntered out of the Multipurpose Room very casually, like the whole world hadn't suddenly turned upside down. I could feel Volger's eyes drilling into the back of my head.

The hallway, once so familiar and inviting, was now a river of strangers. Any one of them could be in league with Volger.

Obviously, I couldn't confide in you. I couldn't be sure of you! Couldn't be sure of *anyone* anymore!

Then I realized that there was one person I could be sure of. One guy in school who was beyond suspicion. The target of Volger's conspiracy. Griff.

I started walking again. My fast walk, the one you make fun of. I searched the busy corridors looking for my former partner. He was nowhere to be seen, but I knew he must be in Rampart somewhere! I resolved to keep searching until I found him, no matter what!

Then the bell rang, and it occurred to me that I might as well find him after next period. I mean, how would me getting a detention help the situation, anyway? It wouldn't. In fact, it would only make things worse.

But I didn't find him after class let out. Or after the next class. Or lunch. I scoured the campus, looked in every spot I could think of. The pitch-black photography lab. The nauseatingly antiseptic-smelling nurse's office. Even the coffee-ground-encrusted teachers' lounge. There was no sign of Griff.

I kept looking. Between every class. After all, a vow is a vow and, as a peace officer and as a person, I don't take that sort of thing lightly. But by the end of fifth period, I can honestly tell you, I'd nearly given up hope of finding him.

"Maybe you need to look where the light's not so good."

At first I wasn't sure if I actually heard it or if it was just an echo from some gravel-voiced cartoon character bouncing around my head. But then I saw him. It was that janitor. You know the one I mean. You never quite notice him, but he's always there. He called my dad by his first name on the day I started here. He's been here forever. He looks like he's made of dust.

"What?" I asked, making sure the voice had really come from him.

"There's an old joke," he said. Yeah, it was his voice, all right. "Dude's on the sidewalk, crawling around, looking for something. Fella comes up and says, What're you doing, man? Dude says, Looking for my keys. Man looks around the sidewalk and tells the dude, I don't see them. Sure you dropped them here? Dude says, No, I dropped them over there. Man says, If you dropped them over there, why're you looking for them here? And the dude says, Because the light's better."

Yeah, I didn't laugh for a minute either. But then I got it. Why he was telling me this, I didn't know. He'd never talked to me before. Or maybe he had and it just hadn't registered. When I'm on patrol, I'm 110 percent focused on the student body. Guys like that custodian are almost invisible to me. I wonder if he's like that to everybody.

I must have had my mouth open again.

"You're looking for him in all the places you usually go, because the light's good," the custodian told me. "When a man doesn't want to be found, he stays out of the light."

Did I *look* like I was searching for someone? Even if I did, how would he know I was looking for Griff? Assuming that was even who he was talking about. Which, jeez, it sure seemed like it must have been. Right?

By now, I was kind of getting the gist of what he was saying, and I looked over my shoulder to see if I could spot a place I wasn't looking. No luck. I knew every inch of that corridor. And I'd already reconnoitered all the usual locations where kids hung out.

When I looked back to the janitor, he was gone. I'd only looked away for like a second! How do these people do this? Do they go to Batman school? Where do I sign up? I mean, seriously, in just one second, no man can just vanish into—

No man. No-Man's-Land! That was it! I had it! Of course I didn't find Griff in any of the usual places! He didn't want to be found! The only place to find Griff was the one place in Rampart Middle where no one ever went.

Not by choice, anyway.

I made my way outside the main building and across the yard. As you know, the asphalt is covered in lines. Game boundaries, free-throw lines, grade-division borders, and the like have all been painted there to bring an illusion of order to recess. As if that were possible. The very nature of recess makes any externally imposed structure impossible.

So, I don't have to tell you where that blue line leads. You're probably wondering if I was afraid. Sure, other kids might have been. When the tiny white particles started clinging to their Scout uniform like snow, they might have wanted to run, as fast as they could, far from No-Man's-Land, far from the playground. Far from Toilet #3 and the knowledge of the Dark Side that came with it.

That's how other kids might feel, Delane, walking into that fog bank.

"Griff!" I called. Not like I was afraid. The other kind of calling. Search-and-rescue calling. "GRIFF!"

I was in it now. The cloud was so thick I could barely make out the compass heading on my watch. Not that it would've done any good; instruments are unreliable in No-Man's-Land. Even with all my Camp Scout orienteering experience, I'd have a hard time getting out of there without those blue lines at my feet. Orienteering, by the way, is the useful skill of figuring out where you are at any time.

"What do you want?" I heard him say. Weird. I could hear him as clear as day, but the sounds of the kids playing back at the yard had disappeared completely. It sounded like he was right next to me, but I still couldn't see a thing.

I whipped around and saw him emerge from the fog. He didn't step out or anything. More like the smoke pulled away from him, opening like a curtain, and there he was. He must've circled me, silently. If so, his ninja skills were good.

I told him. He was right about Rampart, right about Volger, right about everything. But the only way to put a stop to this growing evil was to band together and do it ourselves. The TEAM-UP.

I could tell that he was shaken. Better than anyone, Griff knew what we'd be up against. Maybe this was too much for him. Maybe when they took his badge, they took something more from him. Something that could never be replaced.

But I needed his help. I had to convince him. I spelled it out for him. Calmly. Logically. Two years on the junior debate team has given me a pretty good way with words that I'm pretty proud of. *Of which I'm proud.*

Still, Griff wasn't going for it, I could tell. Perhaps the challenge was too much for him. He was starting to panic! I could see in his eyes that he was about to freak out, so I grabbed him before he could run.

That's when he attacked me. I know, I know, Griff's pretty tough, but when you've trained your body to be a living weapon, as I have through my extensive Scouting martial arts training, no thought goes into it . . . your body just reacts like it's programmed to.

You know, a serious throw down like this one isn't like it is in the movies. There's no slow motion or sound effects of bones cracking accompanying every blow. Dudes don't call out the names of their fancy moves before launching into them with a lot of fanfare.

It's just two professionals, equally matched, going to

town, silently, methodically, matching each other strike for strike, block for block. It's more like a chess game, really, just one for players with a really high pain tolerance.

I won't bore you with the details. I'm not even sure I could. When I'm in The Zone like that, my conscious mind shuts down. Plus, does it really matter who "won" the fight?

What matters is that I got through to him.

If you're reading this, and I handed it to you? That means everything turned out okay and you're completely unconnected to Volger (which is what I would assume, Delane). If Mrs. Nutting handed this Incident Report to you, then maybe I'm missing, or in the hospital, or worse.

But if I'm still walking around the hallways and you're NOT reading this . . . well, I don't even want to think what that means.

CHAPTER ELEVEN

HELEN NUTTING
GUIDANCE COUNSELOR
RAMPART MIDDLE SCHOOL

Continuation of the RECORDED INTERVIEW with seventh grader Griffin Carver.

GRIFF: POCK.
POCK.
POCK.

You've heard the sound a million times. Ten million if you count the echoes. And it always echoes.

I was still pretty shaky when I got back to school the next day. After the Dark Time. I needed to think. Someplace where I could be alone. I knew where I had to go before I even finished the thought.

As I passed Rampart's outbuildings, the white fog seemed to stretch out and welcome me. You can only hold your breath so long. I inhaled and felt the chalk dust rush in and nestle in my lungs and I wondered how many years it would take off my life somewhere down at the end of the line. I might want those years, someday, when I was old. Too bad I couldn't volunteer to give up this one in their place.

It isn't really chalk, you know. That squeaky powder-covered mineral cylinder that you've been using on the blackboard all these years? In all likelihood, it's gypsum. They haven't used real chalk, cool because it is made up of the shells of billions of dead microorganisms, in years. But they, teachers, parents, society, keep calling it chalk anyway. Thanks for the misinformation, adult world.

But whatever it is. It still has to be knocked out of those blackboard erasers. Every day. For every class. That's a lot of gypsum dust. And despite living in an age of post-Internet technological miracles, there was still only one way for a teacher to get those erasers clean. Have some kid knock them together.

It's hard to believe that back in elementary school, kids used to fight to GET that job. What a bunch of suckers we were. Flapping our hands over our heads like our lives depended on it, just so we could swat those bad boys together for Ms. Kozan.

In middle school, it's always a punishment. Trouble-makers are banished to a secluded corner of the yard, where they stand, banging erasers together and filling the air with so much dust that no wind will ever blow it away completely. It's like foggy London town in the really old movies, but I've only ever heard it called No-Man's-Land.

Most kids are afraid of No-Man's-Land. I don't know why. Same reason we're afraid of the dark, I guess. But walking into the billowing cloud of mineral particles felt great to me. Sure, I wasn't completely alone. The shadowy forms of middle-schooler zombies would emerge from the fog and then vanish into it as I walked by. They never talk or make eye contact. I don't know if it's the shame of being in trouble or the fear over what their parents are going to say later when they find out. Whatever it is, they've got a lot on their minds.

That's why I was surprised to hear his voice. Tommy, I mean. It isn't that his voice is so recognizable; it's just who else would be yowling my name across No-Man's-Land like a lost kitten? I figured he'd stop soon enough.

I was wrong. Tommy kept calling and calling.

"Griff!" he called. "Griff, where are you?"

I was starting to feel bad for the eraser clappers. Thought I'd better make an appearance, just to shut him up.

"What do you want?" I asked him. He jumped, of course. I must've looked like a ghost coming out of the fog like that.

When he finally pulled himself together, he answered, "You were right."

"I know," I said.

"Yeah." Tommy nodded. "But now I know too. Aren't you going to ask me how I know?"

"From your wet hair and the smell of industrial lavatory cleanser, I'd say you asked too many questions. Questions some people didn't like."

"You're good, Griff." Tommy shook his head. "I'll give you that. I just wanted to say . . . sorry . . . for thinking you're a criminal or whatever."

"Okay, you said it," I answered him dismissively. "Thanks for stopping by." I could tell he was waiting for something. Forgiveness, maybe.

"It's—it's just . . ." he stammered, "what I overheard in the cafeteria? When you were talking to Volger? It sure made you sound like you were—"

"Dirty," I snapped. "It was supposed to, genius. Do you still not know what that was all about?"

Tommy shook his head. "I'd probably have figured it out if I heard the whole conversation, but there was a lot of static."

"Then let me enlighten you, Patrolman. Belton was a punk, a pushover. I knew it as soon as I heard how loud he yelped when my rubber band nailed him. I didn't even have to fish much before he was offering me the moon to let him go. Said he was connected up the wazoo. Whatever I wanted, his *friends* could get for me. Sky's the limit. Middle school would be my oyster.

"He wouldn't spill then and there, of course. Wouldn't name names that easily. But I knew he'd lead me to 'em if I was patient. So I told him I was interested and cut him loose."

Tommy looked at me, amazed. I was half afraid he was going to slap his forehead and say that if it was a snake, it woulda bit him. "So," he said, figuring it out as he spoke, "you let the little fish go in order to get to the big fish."

That part was so obvious, I didn't even respond to it.

"Figuring out who the big boss was turned out to be no great shakes. Doesn't take a big Sherlock Holmes detective brain to tail a guy for a day or so. I didn't even have to wait that long. Belton was so shook he didn't wait two periods before he went crying to Volger. I'd love to tell you that I thought, Aha! I knew it all along! Could tell he was guilty from the fluorescent teeth. But no such luck. Maybe I wasn't as shocked as the general student population would've been, but I raised an eyebrow over it.

"Next, I followed up that glamorous legwork with a few more days of wearing the treads off the bottoms of my shoes. I needed as much intel as possible before I made my move. Guess you were there when that curtain went up.

"Volger wasn't hard to find, since he practically owns that cafeteria table. I stared down Volger's two goons, Gabe and Boca—"

"Ben and Morgan," Tommy offered without being asked.

"Great. If I ever need to invite Volger's muscle to my birthday party, now I know their first names. Anyway, I let him know that I was interested in his organization. He played it really cool, of course. Told me he hardly knew Belton and besides, 'I can't be held responsible for every random comment made by each and every one of my supporters.'

"'But you do take a lot of responsibility for some of your supporters,' I told him. 'Nino Coluni, for instance.'

"'What about him?' Volger asked. No attitude from Volger this time. I'd hit a nerve.

"'He's one of your biggest supporters,' I said, rather

obviously. 'A big chunk of students will vote however he tells them to. At least, as long as he's on the team they will. It's a shame he's academically ineligible to play, huh?'

"'Yeah,' Volger agreed, not smiling.

"'You know, I had a little chat with Nino. Not the sharpest Crayola in the pack of ninety-six crayons, and that's the one with the built-in sharpener. You ask me, the real surprise is that he got passing grades as long as he did. Especially in Intro to Spanish, his arch-foe class.'

"'So, I did a little checking,' I went on. 'Turns out every time Señor Olsen threw a pop quiz in Nino's class, the fire alarm rang a few minutes later. Everyone marched out of the school and the test was rolled to the next day, after Nino got a sneak preview of the answers, compliments of some slow exiter who hung around Señor Olsen's room long enough to memorize the test.'

"'What's that got to do with me?' Volger growled.

"'Well, when my idiot partner told me that the only action in the last six weeks of school was a rash of false fire alarms, I said to myself, 'Griff,' I said, 'these Hallway Patrol boys've got this corridor locked up as tight as the nurse's medicine cabinet. Who's pulling that alarm?' Answer: Only someone with a hall pass would even have access to the fire alarms . . . a hall pass as phony as Señor Olsen's hairpiece.'"

"By the way," interjected Tommy, "I totally *get* why you said 'idiot partner.' So Volger would think you're bad like him, right?"

"Sure," I answered unconvincingly.

"But why not just bust him?" Tommy asked. "Tell Delane, Sprangue, someone?"

"As I'm sure you're now painfully aware, Volger couldn't be better connected. And I had nothing. No proof. No witnesses."

"You needed him to make you part of his gang so you could collect evidence!" This was a eureka moment for Tommy.

"That was the idea. Anyway, Volger just sat there at his table glowering at me with those luminous teeth. 'Think you're pretty smart, don't you?' he asked.

"'No,'" I told him. 'Janet Creelman is smart. All I did was ask a couple of discreet questions.'

"'I was sitting in class every time that fire alarm got pulled!' Volger insisted. 'You can't tie anything to me.'

"'A little advice, Marcus,' I said calmly. 'Anyone else ever asks you about this, it would look weird if you knew exactly when every single fire alarm was pulled. And second, I'm not trying to tie anything to you, chief,' I said. 'That's the point.' Now it was my turn to smile. 'I'm trying to help you. I'm trying to be your friend. If I could figure this out, it goes to show that someone else could as well. A smart kid might find it helpful to have a hall cop on *his* side. A guy who'll look the other way, tell him when the heat's on. For a price.'"

"Then what happened?" asked Tommy.

"Nothing," I answered. "Then I picked your microphone quarter off the floor and took off. Then he used you to get me booted off the squad."

Tommy winced. I don't know if it was from guilt or embarrassment. "But why did Volger set you up? Why didn't he make a deal with you? You were a pretty convincing creep," Tommy said.

"To you, maybe," I conceded. "You take everything at face value. Volger made me in a second. Everything out of Volger's mouth is a lie. He naturally assumed I was lying as well. And he was right."

"What are we gonna do?" he wondered.

"Nothing to do," I explained. "I'm just another student now. All I can do is keep my head down. Eventually, Volger will probably build me a nice little frame, plant stolen test answers in my backpack, something like that. Sprangue will get an anonymous tip and I'll have a one-way ticket to a new school. Maybe next time I'll be smart enough to really join the marching band."

He rolled that around in his skull for a moment.

"No." Tommy shook his head in disbelief. "No way! No way!"

I'd had enough. The last thing I needed was to watch Tommy have a temper tantrum. I walked away from him.

Then BAM! Out of nowhere, he grabs me! I guess it was supposed to be a tackle, but it was more of a hug. And as my aunt Barb will tell you, I'm not a big fan of hugging.

"You're not going anywhere!" Tommy shouted. "We're going to fight this thing! We've got to!"

"Hands off, Camp Scout!" I warned, but he only gripped me tighter. You only get one warning. I jerked my head down, driving my forehead down onto his nose. I interpreted that high-pitched yelp I heard as a warning to step back before I got nose blood and snugger juice in my hair.

Surprisingly, Tommy wasn't finished. After wiping his nose, he sneered at me, swirled his arms in front of him like he was doing some kind of interpretive dance, and shouted something. "Windmill arm attack!" I think he shouted. Something like that.

Suddenly, I'm swatting away his arms like I'm in a swarm of mosquitoes. Actual mosquitoes would've probably done more damage, but nobody takes kindly to a dork-slapping.

I stepped past him with one of my legs and crowded him just enough to send him toppling over my calf. A classic Griff move, but reliable. Usually.

Next thing I knew, Tommy was whirling around on his shoulders and head. Evidently, he had a badge in breakin' as well, because next thing I know, B-boy is an upside-down tornado. Some blurry Rodriguez appendage sends me flying.

I don't like this. And I let him know. With my foot. He shouts, "Flying kick block!" or something like that just before our shins collide, turning us into a choral group of groans and mumbled, bottom-shelf swearwords.

"Don't fight me!" Tommy shouted. "Help me fight them! I need a partner!"

"You need the school psychologist!" I barked back at him. "There's no way to fight them. They're everywhere!"

"Reverse roundhouse jackal attack!" he shouted, spinning away from me and raising his foot. This was pretty much the pattern of the fight. For some reason, Tommy would shout out the name of whatever crazy martial arts textbook move he was going to pull just before he executed it.

I caught his ankle with one hand in mid-kick and twisted, sending him tumbling across the asphalt and smearing the chalk of a hopscotch grid. He spun when he hit, scooping up a long-forgotten jump rope. By the time he rolled to his feet, he was whirling it around him. Suddenly, I felt the nylon rope encased in dozens of colorful plastic macaronis wrap itself around my neck. Tommy pulled. Down I went, into a pair of trash cans. Or, more accurately, one trash can and one recycling bin. Either way, they were both full of stuff I would rather not have bounce off my head.

I scrambled to my feet and ran. Must have felt like victory to Tommy, who ran after me like I knew he would. I raced to the nearest jungle gym, but not too fast . . . didn't want to lose him.

I ran into the maze of metal bars and plastic slides. Had to time this just right. Tommy was just reaching my shirt when I grabbed the horizontal monkey bar above me and let my momentum flip my entire body over the bar. Tommy was now in front of me, of course. We slammed together and the collision sent him stumbling farther into the play area.

He fell against the teeter-totter, stunned.

"Hey," I heard myself ask him, "you okay?"

He looked pretty bad, so, like a schmuck, I went over to help him up. I must have stepped on the lower end of the seesaw, and when Tommy saw that I'd stepped into his trap, he sprang into action, hurling all of his body weight on the opposite end of the board. Yes, I did have a nice flight. Thanks for asking. As I soared toward the ground, I noticed Tommy picking a dime up off the asphalt. Camp Scouts are thrifty.

I was just pulling the jacks out of my back when I heard Tommy shout his war cry. I looked up just in time to see him swinging toward me on the end of a tetherball rope. Those Scouts must give out badges for Spider Powers. I had just enough time to notice the ball itself pressed against his gut. Countless hours on the playground had conditioned my response, which was to hit the ball, naturally.

Tommy immediately soared around the tetherball pole in the opposite direction.

I never had any official training, just an older brother who fought dirty and wasn't afraid to lean onto his elbows when they were pressed into my rib cage. Our relationship had consisted mainly of Indian burns and unprovoked noogie attacks. Those were the good times. I missed them.

Tommy's assault, all bells and whistles, felt like it was being done for the benefit of an audience that wasn't there.

Still, it was clear that he'd spent time practicing. A lot of time. And just between you and me, he was better than you might think, tumblers and all.

All the while, he kept saying that Rampart had a disease and we were the only cure. Stuff like that. He talked like the announcer in a movie preview, but that wasn't what made me mad. What made me mad was that he was right.

I wouldn't have been fighting him at all, except that I was so burned up about Volger's operation and losing my badge. Maybe it was the same with Tommy, I don't know, but I gotta say that it felt good to blow off some steam like that. Lord knows I had enough of it bottled up inside.

Tommy must've felt the same way because he was breaking out every move from the Chinese acrobats show that was vaguely fight related. Sometimes I thought he was doing tai chi.

I guess by this time we'd made some noise, because the next think I knew, some eighth-grade gorilla had me in a headlock. Another upperclassman had Tommy. I guess we'd been too occupied to notice their approach.

Ever heard the expression "walking Spanish"? It's like when some goon's got you by the collar and the seat of your pants and they're half pushing, half carrying you and you're up on your tiptoes like some crazy flamenco dancer.

Well, take it from me, there's nothing an eighth-grade boy likes better than making a smaller kid walk Spanish to the principal's office. They will bust you for any infraction, real or imagined, just for the pleasure of turning you into their personal marionette without fear of repercussion. Just one of the many reasons I am opposed to student vigilantism.

"Well, well, well . . ." Sprangue said it so slowly, you'd have thought he had a speech impediment. We were both standing there in his office, looking pretty worse for wear from the fight. I didn't even know Tommy *could* be disheveled. At least, I think we were in his office. . . . My peripheral vision was compromised by the swelling from a black eye Tommy lucked into. Principal Sprangue was about as happy as I'd seen him, although kicking me off the force came pretty close.

"I'm not surprised at all to see Carver here," he said, "but you, Rodriguez, I must say I'm shocked to find you standing in my office."

Tommy looked up at Sprangue. He had a couple dead leaves on him from when I threw him into the hedges by the back fence. I could tell he didn't like being on the bad side of the law. Odds were he was about to pin the fight on me. I decided I'd back him up on his version. After all,

I was certainly going to be expelled anyway. Why take Tommy down as well?

Finally, Sprangue asked Tommy the question. "Who started it, son?" He didn't even make it sound like a question. The answer was built into the question.

"What, sir?" Tommy asked.

"The fight," Sprangue continued. "Who started the fight?"

"Fight, sir?" Tommy asked. "There was no fight, Principal Sprangue."

I could see Sprangue tense up. Tommy was going off the script. "Carver is a known troublemaker, Rodriguez. You will certainly *not* be held accountable for any trouble *he* caused."

It was like offering Tommy a full pardon. And all he had to do was point his finger at me.

"I understand, sir," the Camp Scout explained. "But there was no trouble."

I glanced over at Tommy. Just my eyes. I couldn't believe it. He was turning the pardon down. Sprangue couldn't believe it either.

"Those eighth graders, Dickens and Green, said they *saw* you fighting." Sprangue was getting desperate now. He was building a case, trying to convince Tommy to throw in with him. I knew from Tommy's steady, resolute voice, Sprangue was wasting his time.

"They were mistaken, sir," Tommy shot back. "We were in the part of the yard where the kids clap erasers. It was pretty dusty there. I don't think those kids can really be sure what they saw. I think my record speaks for itself."

"Oh, do you?" Sprangue snapped back. "Then how do you explain those knocked-over trash cans!?"

"Oh, sorry about that," I volunteered without being asked. "I tripped."

If Sprangue's eyes were lasers, I'd have been vaporized.

I don't think my acting was quite as convincing as Tommy's. I didn't have a theater merit badge, remember. But I went on anyway. "I was just about to clean up that mess when those mean eighth grade boys grabbed me."

"Oh, I'm sure you were," Sprangue answered me. I don't know what kind of requirements you need to work in our local school administration, but I suspect sarcasm is one of them.

"So," Sprangue said, turning back to Tommy. "You're suggesting the eyewitnesses who saw you strike Carver here with safety cones were seeing things?"

I wish. At various points in our little fracas, Tommy turned every innocent playground object he could lay his hands on into some kind of club, shield, or projectile. He was certainly more creative than I gave him credit for.

"No," Tommy answered, "they weren't seeing things." Was he going to fold now that Sprangue was making him a participant? "I'm just saying they're wrong about what they thought they saw. See, after Griff fell over those trash cans, I tripped on him and went flying into those cones. I guess I was still holding them when I went to help him up."

That was that. There was no turning back from here, not that Tommy showed any signs of being tempted. Sprangue made one last pass.

"Rodriguez," he said, very slowly, "are you absolutely sure this is your story?"

"Yes, sir, Principal Sprangue," he said, without hesitating, seemingly as respectful of authority as ever.

"Very well," Sprangue said after a long silence. "You ought to choose your friends more carefully, Rodriguez. I'm going to be watching you from now on. Closely. Very closely."

CHAPTER TWELVE

HELEN NUTTING
GUIDANCE COUNSELOR
RAMPART MIDDLE SCHOOL

Continuation of the RECORDED INTERVIEW with 7th grader Griffin Carver.

GRIFF: "What are you looking at?" I asked a little more aggressively than I meant to. We were outside Sprangue's office and already walking down the hall. Tommy was looking at me, probably wanting some kind of acknowledgment of our journey into Sprangueville.

Tommy didn't say anything. He just shrugged. I think maybe that was the first time in his life that he didn't answer a question with an avalanche of words. That was progress.

"You waiting for me to thank you?" I barked at him. I'd been ready to throw myself under the school bus for Tommy, figuratively, not literally, and he had to go and jump under those wheels with me. I didn't like feeling obliged.

"Thank me for what?" he asked, in a kind of monotone. The kind of monotone people sometimes use when they're doing impersonations of me. But he wasn't making fun of me. I think he was trying to be me.

"Never mind."

For all his bluster, Sprangue wasn't the problem. He was just a nearsighted bureaucrat so desperate to keep his job that he'd never look too closely at what was going on all around him. No, the real problem was much worse. Volger. And his whole secret operation. How far did it reach? Was anyone safe? Clearly, it was only a matter of time before the entire school was contaminated.

"What do you want me to do about it?!" I realized I was shouting at Tommy. He hadn't asked me anything, but I knew what he was thinking. He shrugged.

"I'm not even a hall cop anymore," I continued. "And with Sprangue breathing down your neck, I wouldn't count on keeping your badge for long if I were you."

Tommy sighed. "Then I guess that's that."

"Don't like the looks of this," said a gravelly voice

from nowhere. Well, not quite nowhere. Looking around, Tommy and I discovered we weren't alone.

It was Solomon Groom, the custodian, of course. He had about six rat traps in a wheelbarrow and, from the smell, I'd say he was baiting them with Gorgonzola and peanut butter. "Seen a lot of bad things go down in my day, but never thought I'd see this . . ."

Tommy bit. "Rats in the school?"

"No," answered Solomon. "but there's always some kind of vermin that needs taking care of. It's you. Boys like you giving up. Good boys. Smart boys. Giving up. Don't like it."

"You don't understand," whined Tommy, not even believing it himself. "It's hopeless. What are we supposed to do?"

"Don't know. That's up to you. All I know is, you never regret taking the high road."

Tommy and I looked at each other. We didn't have to say it, but just abandoning the school to Volger put a bad taste in our mouths. He turned back to Solomon. "What if we—"

Solomon was gone. Not an easy trick with a wheelbarrow full of rat traps. Tommy's jaw dropped to its usual depth.

"Like Batman," he whispered.

"What?" I asked.

"*If* we were going to do something . . ." He was asking a hypothetical. But not really. "Like, go over Sprangue's head. The school board, maybe. Or the police."

"*If* we were going to do that," I explained, "we'd need proof. Without it, my story's just that. A story."

"But there is no proof," Tommy whined.

"There's always proof," I said without thinking. Something had sparked inside me. I was starting to feel like my old self again. "You've just got to know where to look for it."

Tommy's face was an uncomfortable mix of confusion and wariness.

Amazingly, he was still wearing the same expression forty minutes later when we were walking into the boys' locker room.

It was empty, but you wouldn't know it from the smell. Hard to tell which is worse, the BO or the flowery disinfectant they use to cover it up. From the adjacent gym I could hear the unmistakable sounds of floor hockey. There were going to be some bruised shins tonight.

"How do you even know he's in there?" a nervous Tommy asked.

"Only two gym periods. And he's not in mine."

I found Belton's basket pretty easily. "Alphabetical order," I reminded Tommy before he could ask.

Rampart Middle's gym lockers weren't actually lockers. We use an old system where the kids store their regular school clothes in these old wire baskets that fit into racks that lock into place. I think the point is to keep your gym uniform from getting too rank. Anyway, I was relieved, but not surprised, to see that Belton used a combination lock on his stuff and not a key. Only paranoid kids put their jeans under lock and key. Not counting myself. It isn't paranoia if people around you really are out to get you.

I turned the combo dial counterclockwise three times to clear it before landing it on zero.

"What are you doing?" Tommy yelped. "That's private property. Illegal search, man!"

"Tommy," I told him, "sometimes, for the greater good, you gotta bend the rules."

"Sorry," he shot back. "Tommy don't play that."

"Did you just say 'Tommy don't play that'?" I asked, wondering if Tommy's parents kept the TV glued on the History Channel or something. Regardless, I needed a ploy.

I suddenly cocked my head. "Did you hear that?"

"What?" asked Tommy.

"I thought I heard a cell phone ringing. Didn't you hear that?"

"I didn't hear anything," Tommy said.

"No, I'm pretty sure I heard a ring tone. And it came from Belton's locker. That's weird, huh?"

"You mean because the school has a strict policy against cells on campus?"

"We do?" I asked innocently. "Huh. Who knew? Well, you know what that makes this?"

Tommy shook his head.

"Probable cause." I grinned at him. Then I cupped a hand around my ear. "Hey, there it is again."

I didn't bother to look at Tommy's face for his reaction. I just went back to work on the combo.

Applying pressure to the shackle, I turned the dial until I felt the first sticking point. I made a mental note of the number and turned to the left. Finding the second number is just as easy. After finding the other sticking points and narrowing them down to whole numbers, you'll find all the numbers share the same digit in the 1's position. All except for one. And that's your magic number. Then you've got to divide that number by four and . . . Well, a few simple math moves and some trial and error later and . . .

Click.

And you thought it was all talking tough and keeping it together in a tight spot. Some long division is required.

I dropped Belton's lock and slid out the basket. If the point of the baskets is to air out the gym clothes, the experiment has failed. The stench of ancient sneakers clung to that metal like mud to a wet dog.

His clothes quickly joined his lock on the locker room floor. I checked the pockets.

"What do you know?" I smiled at Tommy. "No cell after all. I guess that was just a ringing in my ears." Tommy shot me a look.

"But what have we here?" I asked, pulling out the sneakers. Not his gym sneakers. His hall sneakers, obviously. I pressed the button and the little wheels popped out. I noticed Tommy rub his shin involuntarily, reminded of the hallway chase and trash can collision.

"You want to bust him for sneaker skates?" Tommy asked.

"That won't even get him a detention," I said. "We're looking for a bigger haul."

"What are you saying? That we look the other way? A demerit is a demerit." Tommy looked outraged.

"Don't worry," I said. "We'll nail him for the skates and a lot more besides. But not yet."

I held the sneaker skates up to the window for better

light. I turned the wheel around slowly. I saw something. Jammed in between the wheel and the hollow of the shoe was a clumpy granulated substance. Almost like sand. But not sand. I extracted some with the business end of my pencil and showed it to Tommy.

"Looks like he rolled through this stuff."

"What is it?" Tommy asked.

"Maybe nothing. Maybe . . . *everything*. That's what we need to find out."

I pulled a Ziploc out of my back pocket and tapped my pencil against the lip, dumping the mystery substance inside.

"Where'd you get that?" Tommy asked, eyeing the bag.

"Mom gives them to me every day," I answered, sealing the bag. "It's why I always insist on brown-bagging it. Do you know anyone in the Science Club?"

"The what?" asked Tommy.

"You know, the Über-Geek Society," I explained. "The kids who enter stuff in the science fair. The brainiacs."

"You mean the Omicron League?" asked Tommy.

"Yeah, that sounds about right."

The Omicron League, turns out, is a competitive science organization established in 1926 by Dr. Noah Wortham with the goal of encouraging scientific excellence, high-level problem solving, and good citizenship in junior and senior high school students. At Rampart Middle, the collective test scores of the Omicrons so improve the academic performance index that they are given a great deal more latitude than most clubs.

For example, when we found them after school, the Omicrons were in the science lab. No big surprise there. But the fact that they had blacked out the windows, hung a DO NOT DISTURB—GENIUSES AT WORK! sign on the door, and weren't required to have a faculty adviser . . . that was an eye-opener.

I knocked on the door.

"Griff!" Tommy whisper-shouted, pointing at the sign.

I ignored him and knocked again. Not so polite this time. I was rewarded by the appearance of a face at the door.

"What's the matter? Can't you read?" the girl asked. Then she looked us over and added, "Oh, you're with Tommy Rodriguez. I suppose that answers *that* question."

I shoved my foot in the door before she could slam it shut. That wiped the smirk off her face.

"Hi, Kyoko," said Tommy, wisely jumping in before I could say something inappropriate. "Sorry to bother you.

Griff here just has a quick question for you guys."

"Griff Carver?" Kyoko asked. She looked at me again. I couldn't tell if she was impressed or amused. "You better come in."

I'd been in the lab before, of course, dissecting fake latex worms. So I thought I knew what to expect. Not quite. Evidently, many of the Omicron League's experiments require the cloak of darkness. Stepping in there was like stepping into a cave. A cave full of lasers, bubbling beakers, and computer desktops projected onto the walls. It was a mad scientist's dream. Or nightmare.

"Elias," the science girl called to a lab-coated kid, "we have a visitor. Griff Carver." I won't waste your time describing this kid. I'm confident you've seen one just like him at your school.

Elias put down the laser pointer and looked me up and down like a specimen. "Interesting." He didn't introduce himself or shake my hand or anything. In retrospect, maybe Dr. Noah Wortham should've included basic social skills in the Omicron League's goals.

"We can't help you," Elias said.

"What makes you think I came here for help?" I asked.

"Process of elimination," he said. "Why else would you come?"

"Maybe I came to give you something," I suggested.

"Like *what*?!" whined the silhouette of a chubby boy lurking in the shadows.

"Neal!" snapped Kyoko. "Elias is handling this."

"Like a challenge," I continued, holding up the plastic bag from the locker room. "I've got a mystery substance here. I don't think you've got what it takes to identify it."

Suddenly, all the Omicrons, the ones I could see and the ones in the darkness, broke out laughing. It was a horrible sound. Some of them laughed through their noses. Some wheezed and then quickly inhaled asthma medicine through inhalers.

"What's so funny?" asked Tommy. I was kind of sorry he asked.

"Your friend here was trying to use reverse psychology," Elias explained with relish, more to me than Tommy, "on *us*. I think you'll find it somewhat difficult to outsmart the Omicrons, Carver."

"Of course," I responded. "I'm just not in your . . . *League*."

It was a weak pun, but it got a chuckle. Science geeks have a notorious weakness for puns. It broke the ice. A little.

"We find you interesting," Kyoko said. "Not only did

you immediately ascertain the hidden social dynamics of the school, but you refused to be bullied into acquiescence."

"Thanks. I think. I'll check my dictionary to make sure that was a compliment." A joke at the expense of my own smarts. They ought to love that.

"Look." I started up my big play. "You big brains have got to know that some bad junk has been going down here, on the down low, for some time. All I'm asking is a few minutes of your hive mind power to analyze a clue and help win the good fight."

Neal, the chubby shadow, snorted. "We're not your crime lab, Carver."

"And even if we were," added another voice in the darkness, "didn't you lose something? Like your badge, for instance?"

"*Fac taceas!*" shouted Elias. I may be no Omicron, but I can recognize "shut up" when I hear it. My best guess was Latin. When the league settled down, Elias smiled at me in that way people do just before they're going to tell you the facts of life.

"You see, Griff," Elias started, "good, bad, right, wrong. These are not scientific absolutes. They're imaginary values, societal rules that have very little meaning in here."

"So, you don't care if there's a criminal element taking over your own school? What would Dr. Wortham say about that, I wonder?"

"Whatever goes on in the rest of the school," Kyoko jumped in, a bit defensively, "we don't bother them, and they don't bother us."

"For now," I mumbled, but it was clear they were not going to be swayed by appeals on moral grounds.

"Let's go, Griff," said Tommy. "These nimrods don't care about anything but their test tubes." It was time for the real thing. I had pretended to turn and follow Tommy out when I "spotted" something on the floor.

"Hey," I said to him. "You drop this, Tommy?"

"Drop what?" he said, of course.

"Right here," I said, bending over. It was a simple enough sleight of hand. I wasn't really trying to make it convincing. I "picked up" the card.

"Looks like some kind of playing card," I told him innocently. I showed it to him, pretending to be puzzled. "I don't recognize the suit."

"That's because it's not from a regular deck of cards," Tommy volunteered, very obligingly. "That's from one of those CCG decks."

"From what?" I asked, all innocence.

"A collectible card game!" Neal snorted, moving

closer to examine the card. "Anaxagoras's beard! That's a Neptune's Trident card!"

His fleshy hands snatched at it in the dark, but I easily yanked it out of harm's way. These guys weren't known for their reflexes.

"Oh," I feigned new understanding, "you mean this is one of those Atlantis X cards. I don't play myself, but I understand that some of these cards are a bit . . . hard to find."

Elias eyed me coldly. "What do you want for it?" Maybe it was a cliché that science dudes played CCGs, but in my experience it was 100 percent true.

"Who says I want to trade it at all?" I asked. "Maybe I want to clothespin it to the frame of my Marley Carson and listen to the sound it makes against the spokes when I ride really fast." I could hear the entire group make a collective wince. I was starting to enjoy this. Maybe too much.

"Elias," Kyoko chimed in, "maybe we could help him out. Just this once."

Elias was no dope. Clearly. And he didn't like being played. But he also didn't want to see that card walk out of his little fiefdom. Not with the Ultimate Gamemeister Tournament looming at the convention center next week. It pays to be prepared.

"Fine," he said. "We'll do the analysis."

He reached for the card. I handed him the Ziploc baggie instead.

"First things first." I smiled at him.

Elias took the Ziploc and his team sprang into action. It was actually pretty impressive. He divided the stuff up into three samples and handed it off to three teams: microscopic, spectroscopic, and chemical analysis. Bunsen burners were lit. Beakers bubbled. Noxious clouds filled the lab and were illuminated by the unearthly light of the spectroscope. The Omicrons discussed their findings among themselves in low tones. Finally, I could just make out nodding heads in the darkness. They'd reached a conclusion.

"Nothing too exciting," Elias said. "Wood shavings."

I try to keep my reactions to myself most of the time, a useful ability in poker and law enforcement.

"If it was a snake, it woulda bit me!" I shouted, pounding my thick forehead.

"What?" Tommy demanded. "What is it?"

"Let me guess," I said to Elias. "White oak."

Elias looked dumbfounded. Let me tell you, if you want a shot of undiluted ego in your arm, shocking a certified genius is a good way to go.

"How'd you know?" Kyoko asked. Of course, Elias

couldn't ask. It would mean there was something he hadn't guessed ahead of time. But I wasn't about to answer no matter who asked. We'd gotten what we came for. I looked at Tommy and gestured toward the door.

"Thanks, Omicron League," I said. "I'm sure you'll be happy to know that your help has been invaluable to the cause of justice."

Just as I was reaching for the door handle I heard a snort ring out followed by a wheezy voice. "Hey! What about the Neptune's Trident card?"

I slipped the card between my index and middle fingers. "Here," I warned, then flipped it toward the irritating sound of Neal's voice. The card soared like a Frisbee. A paper-thin Frisbee with four corners.

"Ow!"

I smiled. The allowance I'd spent on that card trick book in fourth grade was money well spent. Tommy and I were already back out in the hall when we heard Kyoko call after us.

"Good luck!" Maybe, just maybe, there was a human heart beating in that room after all. But there was no time to dwell on that. I knew what we had to do, even if Tommy didn't.

"I don't get it," Tommy said. "How does knowing Belton had pencil shavings in his shoes help us?"

"Not shavings," I corrected. "Pencils are made from juniper or cedar. Besides, if there was any graphite, you can bet the Dork Society in there would've told us. Smugly."

"If that stuff didn't come from a spilled pencil sharpener, then what . . ." Tommy's voice trailed off. Then he suddenly snapped his fingers. "Sawdust!"

"Bingo," I congratulated him. "Now, why?"

I could hear the gears turning in Tommy's skull, but nothing was coming out.

"Where do you think Volger's gang got those phony hall passes?"

"Hall pass*es*?" Tommy repeated, stressing the *s*. "You think there's more than the one Belton had?"

"Lots," I answered. "Some they sell, of course. But mostly they're used to buy 'favors' from unsuspecting chumps. Anyway, where would you think they'd get these forgeries?"

"Same place you get everything. From eBay, of course," Tommy answered.

"That's what I thought. Or, more accurately, didn't think. I just assumed the bogus passes were bought online. But think about it. Rampart's hall passes have been around forever. They're pretty unique. How would you go about ordering a copy?"

"You wouldn't," concluded Tommy. "You'd have to make them yourself."

"How?" I asked him.

"Well . . ." Tommy thought aloud. "You said these things were nearly perfect counterfeits. You'd need a table saw, belt sander, stain, varnish. There're probably only a handful of students who have dads with basement workrooms like that. Should we check them out?"

"Wait a minute," I suggested. "How do you know about those workrooms? Those dads?"

"Oh, you know," said Tommy, "they're the super-involved dads. They build the Rampart Middle's Hallow-een Haunted Hovel, the theater sets, stuff like that."

"And the kids of those dads . . . would they be part of Volger's operation? Do they fit the profile?"

Tommy shook his head.

"I think this is an inside operation," I told him. "Entirely inside."

This time the hard drive in Tommy's skull booted up. "Griff, are you telling me," Tommy started incredulously, "that those forgeries are being made—"

"Uh-huh."

"—Right under our noses—"

"You got it."

"—In Rampart Middle's own—"

"That's what I'm saying."

"—WOOD SHOP!?"

They had guts. You had to give them that. But a tip of the hat was all they were going to get from Tommy and me. It was time to flush them out. It was going to take guile, guts, and a lot of luck. But only a sucker counts on luck. Better to have a plan. And one was starting to form, right in the back of my skull.

"What are we going to do!?" Tommy wondered desperately. The depth of Rampart's contamination was almost too much for him.

"Right now," I suggested, "you're going to contact Our Lady of the Press with one of your famous 'insider tips' before the paper is put to bed."

"Huh?" cried Tommy defensively. "What makes you think I tell Verity anythi—"

"Relax," I told him before he could wig out about it. "This is one story that needs to be told."

CHAPTER THIRTEEN

HELEN NUTTING
GUIDANCE COUNSELOR
RAMPART MIDDLE SCHOOL

Continuation of the RECORDED INTERVIEW with seventh grader Griffin Carver.

GRIFF: "No, you're the Man!" he shouted. Undeserved laughter followed.

The nauseating, unmistakable sounds of campaigning echoed down the east hallway, and that could mean only one thing.

"He's coming," I said to Tommy. "Ready?"

"I'm cool," Tommy said.

"Don't be cool," I told him. "Be yourself. That's the

only way this is going to work." I folded the newspaper carefully.

Tommy nodded while I checked around the corner with my dentist's mirror.

"Where'd you get that?" asked my partner, impressed.

"Ninety-Nine Cent Store."

"Pretty cool," he said. "How much did you pay for it?"

I didn't answer him. Instead, I watched in the tiny round mirror as Marcus Volger approached his locker and opened it. He smiled and nodded at a few passersby, but for once, he was alone. I gave Tommy the signal and he started out. I stopped him.

"Don't forget this," I told him, handing him a copy of the *Liberty Bell*. He laughed sheepishly.

Tommy leaned his back against the locker next to Volger. Mr. Cool, just like I told him not to be but knew he would anyway.

"Why, Tommy!" Volger said welcomingly. "How's Rampart Middle's top cop?" He said all this without irony, like they were BFFs. I had to hand it to him, he doesn't show his hand. "How many times are you going to vote for me, Tommy?" Volger asked, laughing at his own oily charm.

Tommy wasn't about to play along. "You're not

going to win, Marcus," Tommy told him. And to prove his point, he showed Volger the *Bell*'s headline:

POLLS SHOW CREELMAN & VOLGER NECK AND NECK

"Your scare tactics are not the best, Tommy." Volger smiled back at him. Of course, I couldn't actually see the smile through Tommy's Spy Bling earphone, but I could hear it. "You tell me I'm going to lose and then give me a newspaper that says I've got an even chance of winning. And let me tell you something. I will win, because I am a win—"

Suddenly, something distracted him. And I was pretty sure I knew what that something was. I heard the newspaper rustle over the microphone hidden in Tommy's badge. There was a long pause. I knew he was reading.

"It doesn't matter," barked a desperate Tommy. "Even if you do win, you'll be exposed sooner or later. You and your goons."

"What?" Volger responded, lost in thought. Finally, he seemed to come to himself. "I have no idea what you're talking about. If you had some kind of misunderstanding with people I know, with Ben and Morgan, what's that got to do with me? And let me just add this, Rodriguez, when I'm class president, I'll have a lot of say over all aspects of Rampart Middle's life . . . including who serves on Hall Patrol. And you're one of the best. I'd hate for you to spend middle school wasting your talents sitting on the sidelines. Remember that."

I watched Volger as he slammed his locker and walked off. It was supposed to play like a threat. But it didn't. He was rattled. Otherwise, he'd never have been so transparent with Tommy. He must have read the article. That was step one.

I pulled back farther into the shadows of the side hall as Volger passed. It could blow everything if he saw me there and put two and two together. Whatever he is, Volger's no dope.

"I don't get it," Tommy said, joining me in the alcove. "What was all that about?"

"Had to make sure he smelled the bait." I showed him the front of the newspaper. He shrugged.

"He knows where the polls stand," Tommy observed, still in the dark. "And really, I don't think Janet Creelman has personality to pull off an upse—"

"Not the headline," I told him, pointing to another article. "Here."

Tommy checked out the less-than-sensational piece.

IA WING REVAMP RAMPING UP

According to inside sources, the long-promised improvements to the Industrial Arts Building have finally moved off the drawing board and, shockingly, been swiftly put on the launchpad. The unsubstantiated rumor has it that the auto, metal, and wood shops could be shuttered as quickly as tomorrow in preparation for the sorely needed renovations. Questions linger as to why the school board would depart from its usual modus operandi of foot dragging and delay to move this project along so quickly, but reliable contacts report that . . .

"It's that story you told me to give Verity." Tommy shrugged. "So what?"

"So, everything. Your relationship with Rampart Middle's top journalist just gave us a chance, a small chance, of maybe, just maybe, coming out of this mess in one piece. If you've got the guts."

"Relationship?" barked Tommy defensively. "Verity's just a friend! I like her, but I don't *like* her, like her. Come to think of it, I don't even like her that much! Heh . . ." Then Tommy trailed off, suddenly hearing the rest of it. "What do you mean '*in one piece*'?"

"Meet me back here at seven tonight and find out. Unless you're scared."

"Scared?!" yelped Tommy. "Are you kidding?"

Yeah. I was kidding. Actually, I was just making sure he'd show up. I didn't think for a second that Tommy

Rodriguez was scared. But I wasn't about to tell him that. I just shrugged.

"I'll be here, Griff," he said with attitude. "Count on it." Then after a moment's reflection he added, "What am I going to tell my 'rents?"

I just shook my head like I couldn't believe how lame he was for having to come up with an excuse for his folks.

What I didn't say is that I was already wondering the same thing. I wasn't sure going back to the "extra band practice" well was a good idea. The Old Lady was going to realize that I wasn't in the marching band at some point. Most likely at a football game. She was already asking too many questions. Why wasn't I practicing? What songs would we be doing? Any eighties New Wave? I don't like lying if I can avoid it. I'm sure even I've got a "tell," some little mannerism that clues the Old Lady in on when I'm bluffing. And I'd rather not have her get too acquainted with it.

I brainstormed excuses all the way home, and by the time I parked the Marley Carson, I had a nice selection of alibis to choose from. I can be pretty creative when I have to be. Not that you could tell from any of the macaroni mosaics I've done in art class. The last one was a representation of a crime scene. I used manicotti for the chalk outline of the body. Got a D+.

Turns out I needn't have bothered worrying about the alibi. Mom had left a note. She had some kind of meeting that night. I didn't read the note in its entirety. I know how to defrost frozen pizza.

Not that I was going to be dining at home anyway. I changed into my nocturnal ops gear and yes, by that I do mean black jeans and a dark hoodie. And no, I don't wear a knit black hat or put football player war paint under my eyes.

It's not like the Old Lady just leaves me alone all the time. Don't call social services or anything. First of all, I'm not a kid, and second, technically, I'm not alone. The Creature is right upstairs, barricaded in his room.

I put the pizza in the oven before I left. Not 100 percent sure the Creature still has what it takes to feed itself.

Tommy was right on time for the rendezvous at the flagpole. I cut him some slack and decided not to give him any flak for the head-to-toe camo ensemble. Just for the record, camouflage only works as camouflage when you're surrounded by similar shapes and colors. Like trees or bushes or desert rocks or whatever. It does not blend in with linoleum.

The door wasn't locked. There's always something going on at night. Play rehearsal or Math Club. Something.

Inside, everything looked weird. The lights for the main hallway might have been on, but that was it. The classrooms were dark, as were most of the side hallways. I wasn't the only one to notice.

"This is pretty creepy," Tommy observed. "I mean, it *would* be . . . to someone prone to—"

My hand clamped over Tommy's mouth at the same time I slammed him against the wall in the unlit south hallway. I'd heard the unmistakable sound of high heels on a hard surface and acted instantly. Two sets of shoes. No, three. And approaching fast. Another second and they would've seen us.

"What—?" Tommy started to ask when I'd released my grasp.

"Mothers," I said in a low voice, then gestured him to shush. The clacking heels were getting closer and we could hear their voices now. It was the conversation about how the teachers, as good as they were, just weren't making us kids work up to our potential. A classic.

As soon as they were out of earshot, I gave Tommy the signal and we stealth-walked across the main corridor toward another darkened wing. Then I heard laughing. Behind us. We only had seconds. I shoved Tommy ahead of me and did a shoulder roll into the shadows. We waited.

Another pod of moms. I knew we hadn't been spotted because the flow of their conversation didn't change. It was about Mr. Knutz, the new math teacher. I don't know who Colin Firth or Pierce Brosnan are, probably soap stars, but I doubt very much that Knutz looks anything like them. As their giggling receded down the hall, Tommy started to advance and I had to push him back against the wall to avoid another stream of parents. A few dads were along this time. They were comparing the warranties on their minivans.

"Too many of them," I whispered.

"Where are they all coming from?" Tommy asked breathlessly.

"The parking lot, probably," I sniped. "Smells like a PTA meeting. Should've checked the school calendar. It's right up on the fridge, too."

Tommy borrowed my dentist's mirror to peer around the corner. "The hall's full of 'rents now," he said. "We'll have to go around."

"Can't. This'll be the only open door. They don't want parents roaming around free."

"Wood shop's on the other side of the auditorium," Tommy pointed out needlessly. "There's no way to get past them unseen. We'll just have to blow off the stakeout for tonight."

"Yeah, only problem with that is," I reminded him, "the trap is set for tonight."

"Right." Tommy nodded. I could tell he was itching to say something else, but something was stopping him. Turned out that something was embarrassment. "What trap?" he finally croaked out.

"The article?" I led. "The story about the school closing down Industrial Arts tomorrow?" I added. "What did you think that was?"

"You said it was a tip," he answered, "for Verity."

"Yeah, that what I said, all right. But it wasn't true. The story, I just made it up. Get it?"

Tommy nodded and I leaned to the corner to see if the coast was clear. No! Almost caught by a silent group of moms. This bunch was sweaty and wearing sneakers. They must've come straight from boot camp. I motioned Tommy to stop.

"So . . ." Tommy realized, "you wanted Volger to think he couldn't use the wood shop after tonight."

It was my turn to nod. "Couldn't just stake out the wood shop every night hoping they'd turn up. We had to force their hand."

"If they think this is the last night they can use the wood shop," said Tommy, piecing it together, "they'll try to crank out one last batch of counterfeits." Nice to see the detective part of his mind starting to work.

"Or at least clear out any evidence," I added. "Unfortunately, when no remodel starts tomorrow, they'll smell a trap."

"And evaporate," concluded Tommy. Now that he knew the sitch, he wanted to punch something. He made a fist and eyed a locker, but lockers are made of metal and would (a) be noisy and (b) hurt. So he settled for punching the palm of his other hand, turning on his heels, and storming farther back into the darkness. Suddenly, I heard a crash.

Followed by a yell. My eyes adjust pretty quickly, and as I made my way toward Tommy's groan, I could just make out a long inverted V beyond the moving lump on the floor I assumed was Tommy.

"What was that?" he asked, standing and rubbing his head.

I told him it was the custodian's ladder.

"Of all the times to leave his stuff out . . ." Tommy murmured.

"Does he do that a lot?" I asked, a weird feeling coming over me. "Solomon, does he leave his equipment out?"

"What? How should I know?" Then, pulling himself together, Tommy amended his answer. "I've never seen so much as a rag left out. I guess that's his way of 'taking the high road.' Always put away your mops, right?"

My mind was racing as I tipped the ladder back up. "The high road . . . *high* road. That's what he said, isn't it?" Tommy nodded. "Turn on your penlight."

I didn't have to ask if he had one. Of course he did. Are you kidding me? "Shine it along the top of the wall, along the ceiling!" He did until I said, "Stop! Right there!" I pushed the ladder across the linoleum. It squeaked. Louder than I liked, but not enough to draw attention. I clambered up the steps to the second rung from the top, you know, the one with the sticker that warns you not to stand on it? There I examined the air vent in Tommy's shaky beam. It was exactly what I was looking for. I pulled at the grid hard, coating my fingers with thirty years of vent dust. No go. It was screwed on tight, like I thought, but it was worth a try.

"Now, give me your Swiss Army knife."

"What makes you think I—"

"Scouts are always prepared," I told him.

"Not this time," admitted Tommy. "I automatically leave the SWAK on the mitten bureau at home when I'm leaving for school."

No knife meant no screwdriver. My mind raced. There must be another way to—then I knew. "The dime!" I whisper-yelled. "Give me the dime!"

"Why would I have change on me?" Tommy asked. "I've got a lunch card. Why would I have a dime?"

"You found one on the asphalt in No-Man's-Land," I reminded him. "And you're wearing the same pants."

Tommy shook his head and reached into his camou-flage change pocket. He smiled and pulled out the dime. "You're something, Griff," he observed, tossing the dime to me. Tommy is a decent throw, which was good, seeing as I had to catch a dime in the dark standing on top of a ladder. I felt it snap into my palm and turned my attention to the grid without a word. Thank-yous are not required etiquette for two guys on a mission.

I really had to work to jam the dime into the screw's groove. It must've been painted over a hundred times. It was anyone's guess as to whether this would even work.

"What's the plan, Griff?" Tommy's voice asked from down in the darkness.

"Don't you watch television, Rodriguez?" I asked. It was a rhetorical question, which means I already knew the answer. Everybody watches TV. "We can't get past the PTA, so we're going *above* them. In the air vents."

I felt the first screw turn under the dime.

"Are you loco, man?" Tommy wondered, also rhetorically. He already knew that answer. "That's only in the movies. They don't make air ducts big enough for people to crawl through in real life. My dad always says that when we're watching cable."

"Your old man's half right," I said as the fourth screw dropped to the floor with a ping. "You'd have to be nuts to install a heating and cooling system big enough for a grown man to crawl through." With a little effort, the last screw gave.

"But," I pointed out, "we're *not* grown men, are we? A school this size and this old typically has a ventilation system large enough for kids our size." I gave a yank on the vent. It still didn't budge, the old paint holding it fast like Krazy Glue. But I wasn't about to give up. Not again. Not this time. Not ever.

I threw all my weight back despite being on top of the ladder. I heard the ancient paint crack and felt the vent break free. I would've fallen butt first off the rungs if I hadn't managed to catch the edge of that little paint can shelf with the slats of the old grid. "Here," I said, passing the vent down to Tommy. "Now give me a leg up."

There was silence down below. I waited, pretty sure I knew what was coming. I was right. "I don't know," whined Tommy. "Running in the halls to chase a perp is one thing, but *this* . . ."

"Look, Tommy, I know right where you're coming

from," I told him sympathetically, "but let me ask you this: You know the Rampart Middle rule book backwards and forwards, right?"

"I guess so."

"Sure you do," I stated with certainty. "Now, in that entire book, is there any rule that specifically states that students are not allowed to access the Industrial Arts wing via the air ducts?"

Tommy was quiet. Then I felt the ladder wobble. A moment later, I felt a tight grip on my ankles. "On three," he announced. "Ready?"

"Sure," I answered. "Why not?" That was another rhetorical question.

"One . . . two . . . three!"

CHAPTER FOURTEEN

HELEN NUTTING
GUIDANCE COUNSELOR
RAMPART MIDDLE SCHOOL

Continuation of the RECORDED INTERVIEW with seventh grader Griffin Carver.

GRIFF: It was a small, small space.

And dark. Really dark. But that was probably for the best, seeing as these air ducts were installed during the Great Depression and probably hadn't been cleaned since.

My brain told me that the ducts were nearly always metal, but it felt like I was crawling through a tunnel made of hair and lint.

"Gross," Tommy mumbled somewhere behind me.

His penlight cast weird shadows in the tube ahead of me. Thanks. Like it wasn't creepy enough already. I kept moving, inching forward on my elbows and knees, trying not to think about the walls around me. They felt like they were getting closer. And closer. Maybe they weren't, but it sure felt that way.

A few minutes (or was it hours?) later, I could hear voices. Even though I couldn't make out the words at first, I was already bored. I knew it must be Sprangue. Ten more feet of cramped aluminum piping and I could see him through the grid as I looked down into the auditorium. ". . . The donations from community leaders and local businesses are helpful to be sure, but the rest of our budget has to be made up by concerned parents such as yourselves! You wouldn't be here if you didn't care. And you know your children's future is the best investment you can make. . . ." Man, and I thought Father Donavan knew how to put the touch on a crowd of parents. Turns out he was strictly an amateur compared to Sprangue.

But at that moment, the PTA wasn't the only one getting squeezed. The air duct felt like it was getting smaller and smaller. Tommy must've been able to hear my breathing getting heavier.

"Cramped quarters, huh, Griff?" pointed out Tommy.

"Quiet!" I snapped. "Just keep moving."

Why did he have to talk all the time anyway? What's wrong with just focusing on the task at hand? Nobody was asking him to talk! Why couldn't he just be cool for once!

"Griff?" I heard him ask. "You okay?"

"Just peachy," I said through gritted teeth.

"It's just . . ." He hesitated to say it. "You're breathing funny. I think you're hyperventilating."

Hyperventilating in the ventilation system. Felt like there was joke in there, ready to be used in a sharp comeback, but I couldn't keep my head straight to come up with it.

"I'm fine." I finally got some words out. "I'm just not crazy about cramped spaces, that's all."

"You must be claustrophobic," I heard Tommy say, kind of. It was hard to make out the words with my heart pounding in my ears.

That's right about when I felt my head slam into something. I probably shouted something the Old Lady wouldn't have liked. "It's a dead end!" I fumed. "This is a complete waste of time! Back up!"

"Griff, try to relax. Take deep breaths. Think happy thoughts. You're probably just at a junction. Here, take my light." I felt Tommy's penlight tap against my knee. I guess I took it. I don't really remember too clearly. Anyway,

Tommy was right. The duct split off into two opposite directions. The little flashlight was just bright enough for me to see that the cobwebs of dust and lint dripping from joints where the duct sections joined together. That explained why I kept feeling weird tingling sensations on my head. I liked it better when I thought it was just my imagination.

"It's a maze, Tommy," I told him in a wave of despair. "We'll never find our way there. It was a bad plan."

"Take the right passage," Tommy said with an irritating confidence. "Then left when you reach the next junction. If we just keep bearing north, we should find Industrial Arts."

"How would you know?!" I cried.

"Orienteering is orienteering," he said calmly. "Besides, I have some familiarity with HVAC systems."

"What?" I said. I started crawling again despite myself.

"That's heating, ventilating, and air conditioning," he explained. "Or climate control, as the old-timers say."

Somehow, I kept on crawling. Just to get away from Tommy's voice, maybe. Who knew there was a thermodynamics merit badge? Who cared? It felt like we crawled through that metal tunnel for days. I know we didn't— my watch has a phosphor glow dial. But it sure felt like it. On and on, through open dampers, up and down jury-rigged detours over sheer walls—it felt like miles. I blew out the knees of my new black jeans. I was going to hear about that from the Old Lady, but that was the least of my problems.

I knew every step (or whatever you call them when you're on your hands and knees) that we made took us farther from the entry point. That much farther from air and freedom.

And light. I noticed that the flashlight, which was never that bright to begin with, was fading. Dimmer and dimmer. Now there was just a weak orange glow coming from the tiny bulb.

"Tommy!" I growled through gritted teeth. "Scouts are supposed to be prepared! Your stupid battery's dying!"

"There is no battery—" Tommy was saying. He went on and on, like usual, but I didn't hear him. Because that's when I saw them. They were just hanging there in the darkness before me.

Eyes.

They were small and red. And angry. I wasn't 100 percent sure they were eyes at first. Then they blinked.

"Rats."

"What is it? Why did you stop?"

"I just told you: rats," I said through my teeth. "One rat, anyway," I said. I was pretty close to the edge by this point.

"Shake it," I half heard.

"The rat?! *You* shake it!"

"No, the flashlight," Tommy said. "I told you, it's self-powered. You charge it by shaking it up. Do it! The rat'll run."

He didn't have to say it twice. I shook that baby like it was a diet soda can I was going to blast into my brother's face . . . er . . . someone's face. With every pump the LED got brighter until I could see the beast. I've heard that in stressful conditions, your imagination can play tricks on you. It can make horrific situations seem twice as bad they actually are.

Even keeping that in mind, if I pretended the beast was half as big as it looked to me, it was still huge and terrifying. Tommy could kiss goodbye his future as an expert on the Vermin Channel. The beast didn't run. It couldn't. It was cornered, backed up against a damper with its louvers closed. It bared it hideous little fangs as the hissing and shrieking echoed through the pipes. By this time, it's possible that some of the shrieking came out of me. Sorry to say.

Then, suddenly, it leaped toward me! I felt it scurry

past me, its little claws scratching at the tunnel's metallic walls. As I may have mentioned, the air duct was a tight fit already, so Mr. Rat had to squeeze by me. I could feel it writhing its way down my side. Finally, I sensed its tail worm across my ankle. But now I was trapped with the damper in front of me and a coyote-size rat behind me!

"Tommy!" I warned. "I think I'm losing it!"

"Don't freak, Griff!" Tommy cried in as reassuring a tone as possible. "I'm on it."

On it?! How was he "on it"? There was a rabid monster rat trapped between us and we were stuck in a tunnel whose walls were closing in on us! At least it felt that way. Suddenly, I smelled something. Something *good*. Something from my previous life, before I was buried alive in the school's climate control system. I couldn't quite place it. . . . Peanut butter! Definitely, peanut butter!

"*Here, ratty!*" Tommy sang. "*Here, ratty-rat-rat!* I've got a delicious extra-crunchy PB&J morsel for you!" I could hear the beast's little claws tip-tapping agitatedly against the duct. It wanted whatever Tommy was selling.

"Come and get it!" Tommy cried. Then I heard a grunt followed by something echo down the tube. I also heard Tommy say, "Ewww, gross!" at the same time that the beast gleefully scratched and shrieked its way past Tommy and down the tunnel chasing the piece of sandwich. For that's what it was: a chunk of Tommy's Emergency Snack.

"Good thing I'm hypoglycemic, huh?" Tommy asked. I'm sure he was smiling.

He was talking very evenly. Trying to calm me down. Didn't matter. It was too late. I could feel pounding against my ribs and the aluminum of the air duct pushing from the other side. "We gotta get out of here!" I don't know if I screamed it or just thought it or both.

"Griff, it's okay!" Tommy said, clearly lying. It wasn't okay! We were trapped with a growing rodent in a shrinking tunnel! How was that okay!? I started to scramble *backwards*, I think. My feet were hitting something. Now that I think of it, it was probably Tommy's head.

"Griff!" he cried. "Focus! Think! You've come so far. We're almost there. Keep it together! Remember why you're here. Your name, your reputation, your—"

"My badge."

"That's right, man," agreed Tommy, "your badge. Don't throw it all away now. You can do this! You can totally—"

"Shhhhhhhhhhhhhhh!" I shushed him loudly.

"You can! You—"

"Quiet!" I whispered. Loud enough so he knew I was serious. "Listen."

As the noise of our voices faded, we could hear

something. But it wasn't a fan or any other part of the HVAC system. It was too high pitched. And it started and stopped.

"What is it?" Tommy asked.

"A lathe," I told him.

"What's a lathe?" he wondered.

"It's a machine," I started, my breath coming back under control, "that spins a chunk of wood around so you can shape it." I could hear that my voice was starting to sound like me again.

"You'd know all about the lathe," I continued, "*if* you took *wood shop*." I pushed myself as far as I could to the side of the duct in hopes of giving Tommy a glimpse of what I knew I could see ahead.

There, not twenty feet ahead of me, light was pouring in from a slatted, rectangular vent. The high-pitched whir of the lathe was coming from there as well.

We'd made it.

CHAPTER FIFTEEN

HELEN NUTTING
GUIDANCE COUNSELOR
RAMPART MIDDLE SCHOOL

Continuation of the RECORDED INTERVIEW with seventh grader Griffin Carver.

GRIFF: Eighth graders.

According to seventh grade legend, eighth graders are given some kind of secret pituitary gland treatment, possibly hormone injections or radiation, which causes them to rapidly double in size. This is not only clearly false, but also probably junk science. I'll have to ask the Omicron League. It is truly said, however, that some eighth graders immediately shoot up to their adult height. It also increases their aggression and capacity for cruelty.

This is not true of all eighth graders, of course. Only the ones who mattered to us. For they were dangerous.

And the wood shop was crawling with them. We could see them through the slats of the vent as we looked down into the chamber. The air duct had widened a bit beyond the grill to accommodate an additional blower for the room. It was just big enough to allow me to turn around. Now both Tommy and I stared down at the busy, lumbering counterfeiters.

Each one of them was working a different machine. The big one—I was pretty sure his name was Jace, but all eighth graders look pretty much alike to me—was at the band saw, cutting out the basic shape of the bogus hall passes. Another one, all pimples and stringy hair, operated the drill press, using it to engrave the painstakingly replicated letters onto the paddles. Dover Belton was there too, meticulously staining and artificially aging the wood by soaking it in what looked like tea and then scribbling on it in permanent Magic Marker. Messy work.

"There's our old friend," whispered Tommy. "That shirt is ruined."

"The seventh grader always gets the worst job, even if he's the kingpin's lieutenant."

It was the best time of all. Time to get down to business.

But before that could happen, words needed to be spoken. I didn't like it much, but the air needed to be cleared.

"Tommy, about what happened back there . . ." I started. I wasn't much good at apologies or thanks, but nobody said life was going to be easy. Or if anybody did say that, they were full of it. "I guess I kinda freaked—"

"What are you talking about?" Tommy said, interrupting me. It wasn't really a question.

"Back there, where the duct got tight—" I started to explain. I never finished. He cut me off again.

"Nothing happened back there, Griff," Tommy said, looking at me steadily. "Nothing happened at all," he reiterated, very seriously. I knew he meant it. My freak-out was going in the vault. No one would ever know.

There was nothing else to say. I nodded. Back to business.

"What now?" Tommy asked. "Call for backup?"

"Yeah, right?" I shrugged. "With what?"

Tommy rummaged around in one of his camouflage pockets and pulled out what looked like a plastic lady-bug. It was red. It had spots. The whole bit. But it was a cell, obviously.

"It's a Snuggebug," he explained. "I know we're not supposed to have phones in school, but this is a special occasion. It calls my mom, dad, 911, or Delane."

I suppose he read a lot into the way I looked at his phone. "The only other choice was a bear."

"The look is not for the red plastic insect phone, Tommy," I told him. "This is my 'no, we're not calling for backup!' look."

"But the patrol regulations clearly state that when officers are engaging an equal or superior force—"

"I'm not a hall cop anymore, remember?" I snapped at him. "So don't go quoting regulations to me!"

I immediately regretted my tone. Tommy was in this with me up to his Camp Scout neckerchief. "Anyway, there's no signal," I pointed out in a more conciliatory tone, indicating the screen. "Might have something to do with this metal coffin we're sitting in." I could see he was still a bit unsure. He glanced around the air duct. I don't know what he was expecting to see.

"Maybe I should crawl back out and call from there?"

"Right," I said. "If they pack up, I'll just ask them to stick around until the cops arrive. It's now or never."

Tommy took another look through the grid and put his math powers to the test. "But it's four against two."

I shot him a half smile. "In my book, that means we just have a slight advantage . . . *partner*."

I could see that that had done the trick. He'd go in. But

it'd have to be fast, before he got cold feet. I took a closer look at the grate. That was a lot of screws to take out, especially backwards from the inside. No telling what kind of shape Tommy'd be in by the end of it.

"What's the plan?" he asked, his voice as matter-of-fact as he could make it.

"The plan is to land on your feet, think on your feet, and rely on the element of surprise," I told him.

"What surprise?" he asked, innocently enough.

Instantly, I grabbed Tommy by the shirt and, with all my might, I shoved him forward. As his head and shoulders collided with the grate, his momentum kept him moving forward and he *smashed* through. I saw his legs disappear through the open vent. Somewhere below, I heard the grate clang against the floor. Yeah, I'm not proud of it, but that's what I did. That's what I *had* to do.

I could just barely hear the sound of Tommy's body landing in the pile of cardboard boxes below. It was drowned out by the sound of his screaming. I knew I didn't have much time. I grabbed the lip of the air duct and pulled with everything I had.

Falling through the air, I wrenched my body forward into a front flip. Didn't want to land on my head. Like it was happening in slow motion, I could see the eighth graders turn toward the boxes below, alerted by Tommy's impact with the boxes. I was probably in the air for about two seconds, but it seemed to me that these guys had a lot of time to move. I lost sight of them once my head was past the halfway point and I was looking back up at the rectangle entrance to the air duct. Maybe we were about to be surrounded by huge, hostile, criminal upperclassmen, but at least we weren't in that chute anymore. Thank God for small favors.

I hit the boxes harder than I thought I would. Since I was still conscious, I figured my hunch was right about the boxes being at least half empty. Coach Schnauz, who is also the wood shop teacher, is not renowned for his shipshape work environment. I looked across the crumpled cardboard to the next box, crushed by the impact, where Tommy's body struggled to right itself. I'd taken a big chance. If he'd gotten the wind knocked out of him, he'd be useless in a fight and it'd be all over for us.

Pain shot up the side of my arm where Tommy punched me. A pretty reasonable response to being thrown out of an industrial air duct eight feet off the floor. I felt a gasp of air leave my mouth, the giddy laughter of relief. He was okay. We had a chance.

"Ben! Morgan!" I heard Belton shout. "Get in here!"

The door flew open and two more goons ran into the wood shop. Now I was *really* glad Tommy wasn't unconscious. "Tommy," I said quietly to him out of the corner of my mouth, "forget what I said about not quoting regulations. You should do that."

But he wasn't listening to me. He was staring at the two newcomers to the party. He recognized them. Tommy's eyes narrowed like a man with a score to settle. We were both rolling off what was left of the boxes and landing in our fight stances.

As the startled counterfeiters rushed to encircle us, I realized that this was the traditional moment for a snappy comment. I had a fleeting fear that it might be provided by Tommy.

"Sorry," he said sarcastically. It was too late to stop him. "Didn't mean to *drop in* unannounced." Clearly, there is a danger in unlimited access to television and movies.

"That's a wrap, gentlemen," I announced. I tried to sound bored, like this happened all the time. That's what airplane pilots do. *Nothing to worry about, folks, just slip on those ol' oxygen masks and buckle up.* "Principal Sprangue's giving a terrific speech just down the hall. I wouldn't want you to miss it. Get going."

They hesitated. This was either going to work or blow up in the next few moments. I had to do something. I'd try the snappy comment. "Looks like you guys shoulda stuck to birdhouses and spice racks."

Belton got a weird look on his face, like he'd eaten brussels sprouts (no offense, brussels sprouts fans). Then he shot back the expected flip.

"Carver, we're gonna make a birdhouse out of *you*!" he shouted. Yeah, it didn't make any sense, but his attitude was pretty clear.

"Ben, Morgan," he ordered, "you take the Camp Scout. Jace and Rico, get Carver." The other two were already moving in on a nervous Tommy, separating us. Jace's face broke into a big smile as he stalked toward me. Not a good smile, the other kind. Rico's eyes narrowed as he rubbed his fingertips together. He took his job seriously. "You're gonna be sorry you ever stuck your big nose in here, Carver."

To be honest, I was already sorry. These kids were big and, from where I stood, seemed to be getting bigger with every step closer. There was only one thing left to do: stall. Stall for the most precious commodity of all—time. Fortunately, Tommy gave me a way in.

"You rat!" Tommy hissed at Belton.

"Oh, don't be too hard on Belton, Tommy," I told him, loud enough for everyone to hear. "It's not his fault."

That got a reaction. And not just from Tommy.

"How is it not his fault?" asked Tommy. From the

corner of my eye, I saw Belton nod automatically. He wanted to know too.

"Belton is nothing but a pawn in Volger's game," I explained. "He's just a dumb kid who stepped into one of Volger's traps. A victim."

I could see the "huh?" written all over Tommy's face.

"Belton had a problem. Most kids do. But Belton wanted help, and he went to the wrong guy."

"What was his problem?" Tommy asked as Belton looked on.

"It's right there," I said, gesturing toward him with my chin. "It's the reason he wears two shirts even when it's hot."

Belton's hands immediately went to his throat. He tried covering his neck with the shirt collar.

"That rash on his neck?" Tommy asked incredulously. "What's the big deal about that?"

"It's not a big deal, except in his own mind," I went on. "But it is a big rash. Whatever that skin condition is, eczema or whatever, it covers his chest as well. And he's embarrassed about it."

"You don't know anything," Belton finally snapped at me, tired of being an audience member in a conversation about himself.

"I know what's in your gym locker," I countered. "And

I know what *isn't*. Didn't you notice, Tommy?"

Tommy shook his head.

"A bathing suit," I explained. "Everyone makes such a big deal out of Rampart having a pool. Hooray for us. Only it's *not* such a great thing if you're all uptight and self-conscious about your red, scabby chest.

"That first gym unit, swimming, hung over Belton's head like the wads of toilet paper on the boys' room ceiling. Everyone would be looking at him. Teasing him, maybe. At least that's what he thought. Who knows, maybe he was right. Depends on who was in his gym period.

"So who does poor Dover Belton go to with his problems? Who else: Marcus Volger, everybody's best friend. And guess what? Good old Marcus has a solution! He . . . I don't know, forges a note from a doctor. 'Please excuse Dover from swimming due to his deadly chlorine allergy.' Something like that. And all out of the goodness of Marcus's heart."

Belton stared at me in amazement. How could I know?

"Problem solved, right?" I asked Tommy, not really waiting for his response. "Wrong. Because Volger doesn't have any goodness in his heart. He's always working an angle. So when he needed something, something like Nino Coluni to pass Spanish, he called in the favor.

"Whenever Señor Olsen sprang a pop quiz on them, Belton was to sneak out of class—not super-hard with Coke-bottle-glasses Olsen shuffling through his filing cabinet—hightail it over to a fire alarm, and pull."

"And he used the fake hall pass to get by the Hall Patrol," Tommy filled in. Then, shaking his head, he added, "So how does that make him a victim? He's totally guilty!"

"Oh, Belton didn't want to do any of that," I said. This was total guesswork now. "Probably said no when Volger asked him. Then Volger kindly reminded Belton of the fake doctor's note. You know the penalty for a forged doctor's note, Tommy?"

Of course he did. "Expulsion."

"Volger told Tommy that Principal Sprangue might get an anonymous tip about Belton's note. Dover Belton was looking at a one-way trip to an inferior school district. Parents would have loved that, I'm sure."

"Why not just tell on Volger?" Tommy asked. "If Volger made the note, he's just as guilty. He's in just as much danger."

"Who would believe me!?" snapped Belton, reliving his desperation. "It's my word against his and everyone *loves* Marcus Volger! A hundred students would back Marcus up."

"Belton," I said calmly, "you're not the only kid Volger

is blackmailing. That's what most of these hall passes are for. Sure, he sells some of them, but he mostly uses them to get the goods on poor unsuspecting saps like you.

"Come clean and we'll find other victims. Let us go and we can all take down Volger together." It was as clean a pitch as I could muster. I'm not much of a salesman. Not like Volger.

I saw the gears turning in Belton's head. He was thinking it over. While he did, I quickly scanned the room, looking for an advantage. At least there was stuff at hand. I noticed a nearby heavy-duty shop vac and, near that, an industrial caulking gun. I made eye contact with Tommy, then glanced at the equipment. Did he get the message? Did he understand the message? No time to find out. Had to hope for the best.

"You think you're so smart, why don't you join the Omicron League?" I saw Belton's jaw tighten. His decision was made. "Volger controls everything," Belton said, resolved. "He always has and he always will. Our job is to teach you what happens to kids who think they can stand up to him.

"Hold him, Jace," Belton ordered the big kid while looking at me. Clearly, Belton wasn't going to take any chances with a fair fight. He needed me immobilized. I got ready for a last-ditch Hail Mary move as Jace came for me. It wasn't a sure thing, just a sucker jab that, if Jace was as cerebrally challenged as he looked, had a fifty-fifty chance of working.

Then, a miracle. The thing I needed most, a diversion, was delivered as if from nowhere.

A blinding flash went off all around us. Jace and Rico, bless 'em, looked right up where the light had come from, their eyes wide open, just in time for the second flash. By the time I opened my eyes, the second light blast was just fading away, but I could see the eighth graders wincing and blinking. From their faces it looked like the rest of the gang was seeing spots as well, and the flashes just kept coming.

"Smile, boys," purred a familiar voice from above. "You're my first *real* cover story of the year." Verity was perched on the roof, her legs dangling through the open skylight. She squeezed off a few more shots with her digital camera, but by now, the shock of her flash had worn off and Belton and his eighth-grade buddies were regrouping.

"Get her!" shouted Belton. Not that he had to. Several were already scrambling up the worktables to grab her. I didn't waste any time. I slammed my heel down on Jace's instep and dove away from him, shoulder rolling over to the stand where the caulking gun rested.

"Tommy!" I shouted, snatching up the tool and taking aim. "Shop vac!" Focused as I was, I could just catch, out of the corner of my eye, Tommy executing a spectacular flip over Ben and Morgan, who were closing on him. Gymnastics badge, no doubt.

Verity was struggling to worm her way out of the gap in the skylight. Being mindful of her camera, she took just a moment too long. Rico leaped from the table-top and wrapped a meaty hand around her ankle. As he dropped back down, he unseated her, but still she held on to the window molding. She hung there helplessly as Rico landed on the worktable and coiled for another leap.

I'd only have one shot at this.

Rico jumped, reaching for Verity's leg.

I raised the caulking gun and exhaled, stilling my hands. I pulled the trigger. The sticky adhesive blasted out, arcing across the room and, amazingly, splattering right in the leaping Rico's kisser!

He cupped his hands to his face and came down un-balanced. The entire worktable upended when Rico's body weight hit the corner. Now there was nothing be-neath Verity's kicking legs but kindling and linoleum. I kept pressing tightly on the handle of the caulking gun, dousing as many of the forgers as I could. The sealant is gooey and slippery at first. The counterfeiters were falling on their cans and scrambling up again like they were on a giant Jell-O-filled Slip 'n Slide.

In my peripheral vision, I saw Tommy reach the industrial-size shop vacuum. "Detach the hose from the—" I started, but he was way ahead of me.

"I'm on it," Tommy called as he knocked the flexible pipe from the belt sander. I stole a quick glance and saw him flipping the switches. First, the on switch. I heard the powerful five-horsepower motor roar to life. Then the clincher. Tommy switched the toggle from suck to blow, and that's when everything went nuts.

The shop vac started hurling the contents of its twenty-gallon drum into the air. Tommy aimed the hose attachment like a sawdust bazooka, giving particular attention to Morgan and Ben. Within seconds the entire wood shop was enveloped in a sandstorm of tiny wood particles. It was hard to breathe and harder to see. Some of the sawdust billowed up into the air vent, making that venue even less appealing to me, if that were possible.

By now, of course, the adhesive I'd sprayed onto the counterfeiters was starting to get tacky. And I'm not talking white socks with dress shoes here. I mean sticky. These guys were like human fly strips with the wood particles glomming onto them the way that girls latch onto tall guys during social dance unit in gym. Finding themselves turned into giant inside-out scarecrows seemed to take the fight out of the forgers. Before I knew it, these guys were headed for the door, running from Tommy's sawdust shower and my glue gun deluge like the Olympic sprint team from the Land of the Sandmen. I was just about to join Tommy in a celebration when I heard the scream.

"Griiiiiiiiff!" Verity cried. I looked up and saw the highest-awarded middle school journalist in the state hanging from the skylight by her fingernails. Something fell out of her pocket, a wallet, maybe. It seemed to take forever to hit the floor. She was that high up.

She'd likely gotten an eyeful of that sawdust when she was climbing back up and lost her balance. I heard the snap of the old skylight molding breaking. She was falling.

CHAPTER SIXTEEN

HELEN NUTTING
GUIDANCE COUNSELOR
RAMPART MIDDLE SCHOOL

Continuation of the RECORDED INTERVIEW with seventh grader Griffin Carver.

GRIFF: I dropped the caulk gun. Every thought vanished from my head. There were no counterfeiters, there was no fight, no Volger. There was nothing in the world except the girl, falling through that cloud of sawdust, and my legs, the ones that were suddenly made of lead.

Then I was looking up at the soles of Verity's shoes. Girly but sensible. My hands flew up and then, amazingly, I felt her weight collect in my arms. More than her weight, really.

That seventh grader was pulling some serious Gs with her. But by then my legs were under me, absorbing the shock.

A moment passed before I became aware of the fact that I was still standing. I'd made it. I'd caught her. She was safe.

"Uh, Carver?" I heard Verity's cool voice say. "You can put me down now."

Why was I embarrassed? *I* caught *her*! *She's* the one who should be embarrassed for falling in the first place. Maybe the moment lasted a moment longer than I thought. The world started to return to me. The last of them—Belton, I think (it was hard to tell with the sawdust unitards)—was running out of the room with Tommy hot on his heels. I did what anyone would do in my shoes.

I dropped her. First of all, I had criminals to catch. Second, if anyone was watching, it would make it clear to them that I was only holding Verity in my arms in the line of duty. Finally, it was the only reasonable response to Verity's teasing. Sure, it was physical, but you try going witticism to witticism with Verity sometime. Good luck.

"Hey!" cried Verity, hitting the wood shop floor. She picked up the thing that had dropped out of her pocket. Now that I could see it, I realized that it was pink and covered with hearts. Verity picked up on my puzzled expression.

"It's my di—reporter's notebook," she sneered defensively at me. "Wanna make something out of it?"

"C'mon!" I barked at her. I snatched up a heavy-duty measuring tape and raced out into the dark hallway after Tommy and the fleeing gang.

In the shadows to my left I saw a figure vanishing into the darkness. From the echoing footsteps, I could tell it was Tommy. That meant no one was chasing the huge figure I could just make out racing off on my right.

Holding it by the tape end, I hurled the tape measure at the legs of the retreating Rico. The tape housing arced past Rico's legs before it ran out of slack and wrapped itself around the eighth grader's shins like a Brazilian bola, bringing him crashing to the floor. But there were more footsteps in front of him. And certainly there were more forgers running the opposite way than Tommy could handle.

They were slipping through our fingers and there was nothing I could do about it. Then, suddenly, the hall lights popped on behind me. As my eyes adjusted, I could see a lot of activity down there. Then, ahead of me, those fluorescent tubes flickered on as well and I saw the giant body of Jace plow into the chest of a kid who dwarfed him. He should've seen him—after all, Meat Montelongo was wearing a bright red reflective Patrol belt.

"Where do you think you're going?" a familiar voice asked Jace. It was Delane. He was with Zinardi and Reams. They were pretty impressive in force. Dugan and the rest of the boys were closing in from the opposite direction.

One by one the panicking forgers were grabbed.

Rico was trying to crawl away from one of the uniforms while untangling himself from the tape measure. There was no hope of escape, but, just to be helpful, I let go of my end of the metal band. It instantly ZIPPED through the air as it retracted into the dispenser. If you've ever played with one of these at home, you know that the farther it's pulled out, the faster and wilder it retracts. If you're not careful, it can give you a good whipping.

"Oww!" cried Rico. Belton had managed to evade Dugan's grasp with a simple soccer feint, but he had nowhere to go. Almost nowhere. He made a dash for the wood shop. But that was a dead end. There was nowhere to—

"Griff!" Tommy shouted to me, reading my mind. "The air duct!" I sprinted after Belton, my mind suddenly grasping Tommy's implication. If Belton made it into the vent, he might manage to lose us in the maze above our heads.

I raced into the room. I could barely see through the sawdust fog. It was No-Man's-Land times ten. Then my eyes adjusted and I could just make out Belton's feet disappearing into the hole. Too late! I braced myself. The last thing I wanted to do in the world was climb back into that aluminum nightmare, but if that's what I had to do, then—

"Aaaaaaaaahhhhhhhhhh!" A bloodcurdling scream pierced the air before I had even finished climbing the stool Belton had left there.

Belton burst from the vent, shrieking like he was on fire. I quickly saw why. There was an enormous rat clinging to his hair and shirt collar. He flailed around the room like a madman. "Get it off!" he screamed. "Get it off!"

I suppose I should've leaped to his assistance, but the rat ended up leaping off of his own accord, vanishing into the particle cloud in a chorus of irritated squeaks.

Moments later, I was escorting a shaken and skeeved Belton out of the room. I handed him off to Zinardi, who handled him none too gently, but I only heard this, I wasn't watching.

I was looking at Verity. It was the first thing that passed for a peaceful moment since she'd made her big entrance through the skylight. She smiled at me, very self-satisfied. I knew that smile. It was the smile of a girl waiting to be thanked.

"That was a pretty stupid stunt you pulled back there," I told her.

"Tell me about it. I cracked my lens."

"You coulda cracked your skull open," I observed.

"Oh, I don't think there was much chance of that, Griff. I'm a reporter. We're too thickheaded."

"And stubborn," I added.

"And stubborn," she agreed. She still had that look on her face. She was waiting.

"I guess you think I owe you something now."

"Well, a thank-you would be nice, but I know better than to expect miracles. Oh, and now that I think of it, I owe you a little something."

Suddenly, without warning, Verity slugged me on the arm. Hard. She used the nuggie knuckle. Yeah, it hurt.

"What was that for?"

"That's for making Tommy feed me that false story about the Industrial Arts renovation. As soon as I checked into it, I knew it was a plant. I put two and two together and had a hunch there might be a story in it for me."

"I'm glad you did," I said, not looking at her. It was as close to a thank-you as she was going to get. I immediately regretted it and tried to dilute it with a put-down. "Next time, you better check your facts *before* you run your scoop."

Verity just raised one eyebrow. "Maybe I did," she said mysteriously.

Okay, that confused me. Would she have run a story she knew was false? Why? To help us? But there was no time to figure it out.

"*What in the H-E double hockey sticks is going on out here!?*" It was the last voice in the world I wanted to hear. But not the last one I expected. I looked over and there he was.

Not that you would've recognized Principal Sprangue as the hopping, sawdust-covered figure before us. But his voice was the same. I was later told that the hurricane of wood specks had billowed through the air duct and exploded through the air vent in the auditorium like a dust tsunami. The Parent-Teacher Association were covered with dust, out of their seats, and into the hall before Sprangue could finish shouting, "Remain calm!" Obviously, Sprangue never got to finish his speech. The PTA owes me one.

"Carver!!" the principal screamed. "I might've known you were behind all this! You are going to pay! I'm not just expelling you from school. I'm going to get you expelled from the school district! Expelled from the county! From the state! So help me, Griffin Carver, I'm going to get you expelled from America!!" I ignored his breath blasting into my face and his index finger poking me in the sternum, although either could be considered physical abuse. Instead, I just stuck out my chin and pointed it at him.

"Go ahead and try," I crowed. I should've just kept my mouth shut, but my adrenaline was pumping from the fight. I couldn't help myself. I'd need something to snap me out of battle mode.

"Oh, Griffin." A forlorn voice sighed. From the utter despair in her voice, I knew it was her. I even turned around. It was easy to pick her out from the group of miserable, dust-covered parents, all of whom looked as if they'd been lightly breaded in preparation for frying. She was the one with the tear carving a path through the sawdust on her cheek.

"Hi, Mom," I said. Now I knew what meeting she was going to. Guess I should read her notes more carefully.

Sprangue was still in the Rage Zone, because he didn't even register that he was standing five feet from the mom of the kid he was threatening, not that it would've made any difference. "Your permanent record is going to look like the phone book! There isn't a school on earth that'll even consider having you—"

"Uh, Principal Sprangue?" Delane interrupted. "I think I should get you up to speed on the situation."

"What situation?" Sprangue barked. "I know every-thing that goes on in my school, and I don't need some punk kid . . ." His voice trailed off as he noticed the rent-a-cops and the eighth graders in their custody. Now he looked more confused than usual. Delane took that as a green light.

"Carver and Rodriguez here have broken up a ring of student counterfeiters. They were illegally using the wood shop to create fake hall passes that they'd sell to the student body, encouraging truancy and, if I may say, weakening the moral fiber of Rampart. All the proof you need is right in there," explained Delane, nodding toward the wood shop.

He wasn't about to go further, about how the fake hall passes were just poker chips in a pitiless game of power brokering. It would be amazing if even this much registered.

Stunned, Sprangue stepped up to Belton, just being dragged off to police headquarters. "Is this true?" he asked. Seemed to me that he wasn't so much demanding a confession as begging for a denial. Evidently, Belton didn't understand what Sprangue was looking for, because he nodded, admitting his guilt. Sprangue's face went from confusion to despair. If the principal were a bike tire, I'd say he suddenly lost about thirty pounds per square inch.

But Belton's nod wasn't enough, near enough, for me.

"Tell 'em the rest," I growled as I joined them. "Tell 'em who you work for!" I saw blind panic enter Belton's eyes. Out of the corner of my eye, I could see Jace violently shaking his head, desperately signaling Belton to keep quiet.

"Say it!" I shouted at Rico, then at Jace. "Say the name! Tell them who's behind every dirty, rotten endeavor at this school!"

I was desperate. It felt like I was just a hair's breadth away from vindication. And then I heard it.

"Yes, *tell us.*"

The voice was like a novelty joy buzzer going off in my spine. But with even less "joy." I turned, hoping that I'd just imagined the voice. But there he was. And there was the smile.

Marcus Volger. Like he just stepped off his campaign poster.

"Please, if there's some secret criminal mastermind behind every supposed transgression at Rampart Middle, we deserve to know about it." I don't know how he does it, but everything he says drips with innocence and sincerity. Smug sincerity.

My legs felt like melting ice as some part of my mind became aware that the landscape was shifting. I got in Morgan's face. Everyone was watching. The name had to come from one of them or it meant nothing.

"Your boss is right here," I growled low, glancing toward Volger. "All you've got to do is say his name."

Morgan shook his big red moss-covered head. "I've never seen that kid before in my life."

I honestly don't know what I was about to do. Shove him? Scream? Just totally flip out? We'll never know. Delane stepped in before I could make things worse.

"Griff," Delane told me, "Marcus is the guy who tipped us off. We're only here because he called us."

"What?" I said. I couldn't believe it. It didn't make any sense. I locked eyes with Verity. "But I thought *you*—"

She read my mind. "It wasn't me, Griff. Soon as I knew something was up, I grabbed my camera and headed for the fire escape." She looked as baffled as I felt.

"You see, during my campaign, I've been doing a *lot* of talking," Volger joked. The mostly sawdust-covered crowd chuckled appreciatively. He really was good at this, the lying viper. "But I've also done a lot of *listening*. And when I heard rumors that some sort of nefarious goings-on would be happening here tonight, I of course did my civic duty and alerted the proper authorities. Right, Delane?"

"Yeah," Delane said. I prepared myself. Delane loved that transcript of his. It would be easy pickings to blow his own horn here, leaving Tommy and me out hanging in the breeze. Slowly, deliberately, he turned to Principal Sprangue. "But it was really HP Rodriguez and concerned student Carver here who spearheaded their own investigation and tracked the culprits here to the scene of the crime." He turned to me. "And I *trust* they've collected *ample* evidence?"

I nodded and shrugged toward the wood shop door. "Plenty. In there."

Amazingly, Delane turned toward the fluffy, wood-chippy PTA and played to them. I wouldn't be surprised if he runs for office in high school. "I think we all, parents, faculty, and students alike, owe a big debt of thanks to Tommy and Griff."

There's a collective consciousness in any crowd, a hive mind, and it's a mind that loves a cue. And Delane, bless him, had just given the crowd a cue . . . and Tommy and me a gift. The adults started clapping. There were even a few hoots and boo-yahs. All eyes turned to Sprangue. The PTA clapping was *his* cue, of course. He did not look happy.

"Rodriguez, *Carver*," he said through his unmoving smile, "you *appear* to be a real credit to this school. Please accept our gratitude." I thought he was about to spontaneously combust from frustration. But the grown-ups couldn't tell. They were cheering and applauding. I could feel the Old Lady's eyes on my back. I tried to not look. But, finally, I couldn't help myself. I craned my neck looking back at her. She was clapping too. And she had a big, dumb proud mom smile glued on her face. I smiled too. A little.

Even Volger was clapping. At least he was making a big show of moving his hands back and forth. I doubt he was actually making any noise. But his hateful stare at me said plenty.

Tommy shot me a look. He wasn't done. "Aren't you forgetting something, Principal?" he asked innocently, but with a meaningful glance.

Verity, very professional, nodded at Tommy. Good job.

I saw the last bit of breath escape Sprangue. He threw in the towel. "Griffin Carver," he said in a monotone, "I hereby reinstate you to the Safety Patrol service, effective immediately."

Verity looked right at me and smiled like I was the yearbook photographer. I think I saw all of her teeth.

As you know, I'm not the kind of guy who gets all emotional. If you're not careful, that sappy stuff will trip you up. But I've got to admit . . . I felt pretty good. Real good.

The feeling wasn't even ruined when Sprangue pinched

the back of my neck, leaned in, and whispered out of the corner of his fake smile, "But I'll be watching you, Carver. Oh, yeah. I'll be watching . . ."

Big deal. I'll be watching too, I thought as I stared at Volger disappearing down the hallway. I'll be watching too.

A few minutes later everyone was making their way out of the building. The PTA was too itchy and anxious for hot showers to listen to any more of Sprangue's speech-ifying, not that they were that excited about it in the first place.

As we headed for the minivan, I felt the Old Lady grab my hand and swing it, like when I was a kid. Feeling particularly magnanimous, I let her do it.

"By the way, Mom," I said, because it was eventually unavoidable, "I'm not really in the marching band."

"I know," she answered flatly. "I figured that out four days ago when I asked the band teacher how you were coming along." But she was still holding my hand and swinging our arms. "You should know two things. One, that I'm very proud of you, Griff. And two, that you are in *serious* trouble, young man. You never lie to me. *Ever.* You do the crime, you serve the time. Understand?"

"Ma." I half smiled up at her. "I wouldn't have it any other way."

CHAPTER SEVENTEEN

HELEN NUTTING
GUIDANCE COUNSELOR
RAMPART MIDDLE SCHOOL

Continuation of the RECORDED INTERVIEW with seventh grader Griffin Carver.

GRIFF: It was almost like thunder. Almost. But not quite. It was too rhythmic. Too regular. Da-dum. Da-dum. But like a storm over the lake, it rolled closer and closer. Sure, you could hear it, even if you couldn't quite make it out. But you felt it. It shook the floor. The closer it came, the stronger it shook.

They rounded the corner into the main hallway, a mass of hysterical joy. You could make out the words then. You couldn't help it. No, not words. Word. Just one.

"MAR-CUS! MAR-CUS! MAR-CUS!"

As more of the crowd surged into the hall, he appeared as well. Above them. The new class president was riding on their shoulders. I wondered if that was their idea. Or his. His acolytes were throwing ripped-up notebook paper into the air like confetti.

It was a landslide, of course. Who wouldn't vote for a guy who took time out from his campaign to help bring down a gang of bad kids in his school? Janet Creelman couldn't compete with that. Heck, I would've voted for him. If I didn't know. But I knew.

I could feel Verity and Tommy look at me, but I didn't move. I just kept leaning against my locker like I could care less. I guess they took a cue from me because, by the time Volger's victory parade came marching by us, Tommy and Verity were in pointedly unimpressed poses as well. It's pretty tricky to pull off, looking as if a hundred chanting revelers don't make any impression on you. But they were pretty convincing.

I looked up just once. He must've sensed my stare because, just for a minute, Volger stopped grinning and high-fiving everyone around him and our eyes met. The student council grimace vanished from his face.

Then he smiled at me. Or tried to, anyway. I understood

what that smile was intended to say. It was meant to be a victory smile. It was supposed to say, "I won, I beat you, and there's nothing you can do to me."

But it took just a moment too long to arrive. He hesitated, and in that second, I saw his fear. He knew I would never rest, never forget my mission, and certainly never give up. I would expose him. If it took all middle school, Marcus Volger was going down. The inevitability of his destruction hung in the air between us for a fraction of a second. Then it was gone, in his toothy show of bravado. But it was too late. I'd seen past the armor. I knew he was afraid.

Consummate actor that he was, Volger forced himself back into a fist-bumping mania as the adoring crowd carried him out of my line of sight. I opened my locker and fished out the books for that morning. There was an uneasy silence coming from Tommy and Verity as the chanting trailed off down the hall. They both probably wanted to say something comforting, something I didn't need to hear, but there was no way for me to explain that to them.

Fortunately, another sound filled that quiet void, eliminating the need for their consolations.

Swish . . . swish . . . swish . . .

Solomon appeared, following the same route as Volger's

rowdy supporters. He was pushing a heavy-duty industrial push broom with thirty-six inches of polypropylene bristles. More than a match for the improvised confetti of the unauthorized marchers.

"Solomon," I greeted him, gesturing to his pushcart against the wall. It was loaded down with rat traps. Clearly, he'd been collecting them. "Did you catch him?"

Solomon shook his head. "Nah," he said. "Heard he helped you boys out. Figured that made him one of the good guys."

I nodded to him. He nodded back. Seems to me we were always having a conversation without words.

Tommy, however, was a big fan of words.

"More work for you, huh, Mr. Groom?" he commented, looking at all the election day confetti. Solomon stopped sweeping for a moment and looked at us.

"Nothing wrong with a little hard work," he said. "Makes life worth livin'." Then, looking right at me, he added, "There's a real satisfaction in leavin' a place better than you found it. Wouldn't you say, Griff?"

I half smiled, closed my locker, and headed toward class. Walking away, I called back to him, "I'll let you know, Solomon. I'll let you know."

Tommy and Verity walked with me. I guess their classrooms were in the same direction. Don't know for sure.

It's not like I memorized their schedules. As we made our way through the hall, I could feel the pressure building in Tommy to start talking again. He'd come a long way. A few weeks ago he wouldn't have lasted this long. Anyway, he didn't get the chance. Another voice echoed through the hallway behind us.

"Griff!"

We all turned in unison. It was Delane, surrounded by a few of the guys from the squad. He ignored whatever they were pestering him about and reached into his pocket.

"You left something in my office," he shouted, fishing around for it. He took it out and chucked it across the hallway. It arced through the air in slow motion. Sorry, but it did. To me, anyway.

I casually put up my hand and felt it swat neatly into the palm.

My badge.

I made a point of not looking at it before clipping it onto my belt. It's important to keep emotional scenes to a minimum, especially in public.

"Thanks," I called back to him. My voice didn't crack or anything. I said it like he was loaning me a pencil, then turned away and kept walking.

"I know you said you don't want any kind of

unnecessary publicity—" Verity started.

"You got that right," I cut in. I could feel her smiling behind me.

"—But, if I *were* going to run an article about your triumphant return to duty—" she continued, ignoring me.

"Which you're *not*," I insisted.

"—What message, if any, would you have for the student body of Rampart Middle, Hallway Patrolman Carver?"

I don't know why, but I actually thought about that for a moment. Then, even more strangely, I answered her.

"Walk carefully."

Just then, the class bell rang and the hallway was its usual rush of chaos and noise. We continued on our way, my friends and I, like we had the entire school to ourselves.

ACKNOWLEDGEMENTS

The author wishes to thank, among many others, Jim Rockford, Jane Marple, The Falcon, The Saint, The Hardy Boys, Sam Spade, Adrian Monk, Carl Kolchak, Virgil Tibbs, Joe Friday, Starsky, Hutch, Fred, Daphne, Shaggy, Scooby, Velma, Batman, Philip Marlowe, Charlie Chan, Hill & Renko, Riggs & Murtaugh, Holt & Steele, Jessica Fletcher, C. Auguste Dupin, Mister Moto, Father Brown, Lieutenant Columbo, Chief Inspector Japp, Dr. Quincy, and, obviously, Harry Callahan for their tireless pursuit of justice.

A special shout out to Sherlock Holmes, the world's first consulting detective, whose exploits were read to me nightly by my father. I am forever indebted to my dad for handing down to me his lifelong love of books, mystery, adventure, and especially, always, a good joke.

I am thankful as well to my mother, a fine artist, for making our house, though it was surrounded by ice and snow, a place where creativity, warmth, beauty, and wit were always at home.

My book agent, Richard Abate, has my astonished thanks for bamboozling Razorbill into buying my book.

And speaking of Razorbill, my editor Jessica Rothenberg has been a patient and unflagging supporter, full of excellent suggestions and even greedily accepted praise.

Jessica Horowitz will forever have my thanks for her unbridled enthusiasm, which enabled Griff Carver to pry himself loose from my idea notebook.

I will always pick up the phone for Matt Wayne who, to my knowledge, never screened my calls despite my constant pleas for his wise council.

And just in case I never get to do another page of acknowledgements, thanks to my manager, the Great Andrew Deane, for sticking by me, to John Semper for teaching me how to rewrite, to Joel Surnow for showing me how to break a story, to Andy Breckman for explaining to me that the good time trumps everything.

And finally, my most heartfelt thanks to my family.

Due credit must go to my son Riley who, at age five, balked at the very notion of a cop without a squad car. "Does he at least have a bike? Does it have a siren?" I wish I had your imagination, son.

My little girl, Dalila, gave me constant encouragement in the form of impromptu dancing, unprovoked laughter, and the intelligent light that shines from her eyes.

And especially, unending gratitude to my beautiful and loving wife Susan, who is the central, unsolvable mystery of my life.